BOOK 4 OF
THE YELLOW HOODS

BEAUTIES OF THE BEAST

AN EMERGENT STEAMPUNK SERIES
BY ADAM DREECE

ADZO Publishing Inc.

Calgary, Canada

ADZO Publishing Inc.
Calgary, Alberta, Canada
www.adzopublishing.com

Printed in Canada

This is a work of fiction. Names, characters, places, and incidents are a product of the author's imagination. Locales and public names are sometimes used for atmospheric purposes. Any resemblance to actual people, living or dead, or to businesses, companies, events, institutions, or locales is completely coincidental.

Library and Archives Canada Cataloguing in Publication

Dreece, Adam, 1972-, author
 Beauties of the beast / by Adam Dreece.

(Book 4 of the Yellow Hoods : an emergent steampunk series)
Issued in print and electronic formats.
ISBN 978-0-9948184-0-9 (paperback).--ISBN 978-0-9948184-1-6 (pdf)

 I. Title. II. Series: Dreece, Adam, 1972- . Yellow Hoods ; bk. 4.

 PS8607.R39B43 2015   jC813'.6   C2015-905074-X
                                           C2015-905075-8

3 4 5 6 7 8 9 3/22/17 0

DEDICATION

To my wife, who holds me together
when I start to rattle apart,

To my daughter, who always looks at
me with hope and pride,

To my older son, whose questions and
way of looking at the world is
inspiring,

To my little guy, who reminds me that
victory comes
with bumps, scratches,
and sometimes tears,

And to my unbelievable friends
and fans,
you are still, and forever will be
"All the Awesome."

PREVIOUSLY

Don't remember exactly what was going on in the last few books? Then this section's for you! Otherwise, skip on ahead to Chapter One.

Franklin Watt betrayed the Yellow Hoods, resulting in Elly being shot by Andre LeLoup. Refusing to let her die, Tee pushed herself to her limits and ended up in an impossible situation.

Christina Creangle and Mounira made it to Kar'm, a secret research facility of inventors, engineers, and scientists who are neutral in the war between the Tub and the Fare. However, sensing that remaining neutral could have dire consequences, Christina gave a rousing speech to get everyone committed helping the Tub.

Bakon, Egelina-Marie and Richy were captured by the Lady in Red, and Abeland Pieman revealed that Bakon is her son.

The twisted trio of Hans, Saul, and Gretel found the Hound and took him in, enraging Hans. After burning down their childhood home, Hans came after Gretel.

And a surprise attack was launched against Marcus Pieman at his presidential palace in Teuton. While Marcus survived, Tee's grandfather, Nikolas Klaus, was found unresponsive.

EORTHE

Cartographer: Driss of Zouak, 1793
Created at the behest of the Council of Southern Kingdoms

CHAPTERS

Hounding of the Gingerbread Man 1

Cat's Bel 8

Lost Wolf 19

Da Boss 28

Death of the Hound 36

Pieces of the Pieman 43

One for the Road 50

Watt Shines Brightly 65

Dragon and Fox 76

Lost Beauties 90

You can never go home 98

Max'ed Out 108

Without Regret 128

The Rocket and the Pack 134

Emotional Chasm 150

An Order of Redemption, To Go 168

A Benjamin, Tee'd Up 174

Unconventional Moment 182

Scout's Honor 192

Thinking What I'm Thinking 198

Family Matters 202

Red Hooded Plans 208

The Unexpected 220

Signaling the End 231

On Track 238

Karm'ic Trappings 244

Up for the Fight _____ 248

To Air is Human _____ 255

Journeys Ahead _____ 264

Trained on the Morale Horizon _____ 274

Before the Dawn _____ 279

The World, with a Wink _____ 286

CHAPTER ONE

HOUNDING OF THE GINGERBREAD MAN

In the blink of an eye, the Hound had been robbed of all the confidence and purpose he'd built up in recent months. One moment he'd been reveling in the power of the shock-gloves given him by Simon St. Malo, and the next he was sent screaming as he was struck by the rocket-cart, and splashed by the acid from the shock-gloves' battery.

When Hans, Saul and Gretel had found him the next day, lying there, unable to move, he'd expected they would kill him. Something in Gretel's light brown eyes had motivated him to gather every ounce of strength he had left and whisper to her for help. To his surprise, she said she would take care of him, and then she did.

She'd tended to his wounds for weeks while he laid there, wallowing in self-pity and despair. She spoke to him for hours, and in recent days, he'd started to listen. She was struggling with nightmares, and her own questions of self-worth. Then yesterday, he'd decided to make his awareness of her known. He thanked her, and rolled over, unsure what else to do or say. He'd never had anyone be so unconditionally kind to him.

Gretel's soul-splitting scream traveled down the forest path, into the burning cabin, and into the soul of the Hound. His eyes snapped open. He roared in pain as he tried to sit up and failed. His body was a scarred and listless stranger to him, not yet willing to obey. After a second attempt, he rolled himself onto the wood plank floor.

He coughed violently as the thick smoke filling the cabin introduced itself to his lungs. All four walls of the small cabin were ablaze, with flames licking at the ceiling's beams. Scanning about, he noticed something out of place and crawled forward to get a better look. It was Saul's booted foot, sticking out from behind a toppled table. He vaguely remembered hearing Hans argue with Saul, and realized that Gretel's psychopathic twin brother had set the fire after knocking Saul out.

"Saul," he whispered, his voice raspy. After a long few seconds, he slapped the boot hard and yelled, "Saul!" With no reply, he wiggled his way up to Saul's chest. He put his hand over Saul's mouth, hoping to feel his breath, but he couldn't feel anything. He rubbed his fingers together, unsure whether or not he could feel much anymore. Saul might very well be alive for all he knew.

He laid his weary head on the floor, trying to think.

His lungs and body yelled at him in pain, and a little voice inside him wanted the Hound to just accept the fate he'd asked for so long. But Gretel's scream still rang in his ears.

He glanced up at the burning ceiling. He knew he didn't have much time. Trying to save Saul could mean both of them losing their lives, leaving Gretel to fall victim to whatever horrors Hans had in mind.

Finding the door, the Hound forced his body over to it, moving slowly on his hands and knees. He stared at the knob, so tempting and dangerous. He could hear the voice of one of the nun's from his childhood orphanage scolding him for even thinking of it. Laying on his back, he kicked the lower center of the door as hard as he could. Nothing happened.

He tried two more times without success, and finally lowered his legs in exhaustion. He felt dizzy, and gazed about, hoping for some inspiration. As if solely for that purpose, he heard Gretel scream again. With a roar, he kicked the door handle, breaking the door lock and then rolled out of the way as the door swung inwards. Grabbing Saul, he stood and staggered clear of the burning cabin.

Dropping Saul on the grass by a tree, the Hound fell back on all fours, coughing. His ears were filled with the sound of his blood rushing, but his mind was filled with thoughts of Gretel. "Where are you?" he whispered on the wind. Then, as the first notes of a fresh scream arrived, he was off in a dead run.

———————

Hans laughed maniacally as Gretel stumbled, the fog in her mind growing as the effects of the Ginger-laced cookie he'd given her took hold. He wondered how Mother had come up with it, and if she'd found any irony when he'd turned the tables on her. The concoction's sweet smell hid its nefarious effects, which went from mild paralysis to outright blackouts and memory loss. He'd become a master of it, and had been supplementing Gretel's regular mealtime dose with gingerbread cookies for years.

Telling Gretel that he was the man from her nightmares, that they had been real, was even more freeing than burning down Mother's house. He felt like there was nothing he couldn't do, no one that he couldn't own.

"Come on, Gretel! Run! Run! As fast as you can, but you can't outrun me, I'm the Gingerbread man!" He helped her up once again and then a moment later, shoved her over. "You can't run from the Gingerbread Man? So sad."

"Why are you doing this?" she asked, tears streaming down her face. Her hands and feet had already gone numb, and the ground seemed to tilt every time she tried to take a step.

Hans grabbed her by her long, platinum-blond hair. "Oh, that look, that doe-eyed fear, it's really something.

All those nightmares of yours, they were delightful moments, at least for me," he said, his devilish light brown eyes preying on her. He let her go and gazed about at the silent forest.

Gretel fumbled about, failing to get up. "Why are you doing this?" she repeated.

"Why? Well, one reason I recall," he said crouching down to look at her, "you sided against me. Me, your own flesh and blood!" He took a moment to dust off his clothes and calm down.

Gretel took a swing at him, but missed terribly.

"Oh, please," he said, walking around her. "I can't believe that you chose a broken animal of a man, one that we should have put down, over me. And where is he now?" Hans gestured to the tranquil forest around them. "Did you expect that you could nurse your broken beast back to health and he'd whisk you away? A lost dog turned secret prince?" Hans pointed at her and laughed hard. He wiped a fake tear. "Wouldn't that be rich? The poor little forest girl, who has done horrible wrongs, washes away her sins and is made royal through a solitary noble act. Well, I'm sure sillier tales have been written." He kicked her over.

"You're a monster," said Gretel, returning to all fours. She clutched the ground, as her world was spinning. Her mouth filled with a watery taste as the nausea built.

Hans grinned from ear to ear. "Monster? No, I'm the

Gingerbread Man. Maybe I'll be known for creeping into the homes of little boys and girls and robbing them of their innocence. Yet again, maybe I'll just steal cookies. Who knows? I'm free, so very, very free." He crouched down and stroked Gretel's hair, loving her inability to resist. "It could have been us taking on the world. Maybe it still will. Maybe you'll join in the second act, after you come back to being the real Gretel, and not this pathetic, broken girl."

Gretel fell flat, unable to feel her arms and legs anymore. "Please, stop!"

"Ah, the begging. Are we here already?" he looked skyward, as if the sun would answer his question. "Can you feel the moment coming? I can. It's exciting." He rolled her over on her back. "I'll tell you what. If you don't want to be a part of this, just get up and walk off. I won't chase after you. Come on, just walk a yard and you'll be out of my reach. My Gretel would have it in her, she'd stop at nothing. She was ruthless. Come on... prove to me you don't want this!"

Gretel tried to talk, but her mouth was no longer willing to do her bidding.

"Need a hand? Well, I am a gentleman, after all," he sneered, picking up her limp body. "I'll even give you the first two steps for free." He moved her and then let her go. He crouched down beside the crumpled heap on the ground. "Just one foot, Gretel. Crawl it, walk it, I don't care." He poked her with his finger. "What's that? You want to stay?"

Gretel mumbled.

Hans stood and raised his arms in victory, breathing deeply. "I love the air here! It's so... inspiring. Now, why don't I show you where those wonderful little dreams you have of me come from, hmm?" he said, a vicious grin shining from his dark soul. "I've been waiting for this moment."

"Glad to hear it!" yelled the Hound, tackling him to the ground.

Gretel sighed with relief as she passed out.

CHAPTER TWO

CAT'S BEL

The Lady in Red was quite pleased with herself. She'd been able to pick up Abeland's trail quickly, and after Simon St. Malo's failure, she'd decided to tend to it personally. She'd only needed to wait a day for Abeland to put himself somewhere that would be easy to surround and secure. The small two story inn had provided little hope that he and his companions would escape, but still, she knew better than to underestimate him. He was famous for getting out of difficult situations with little more than a smile or a clever word. She'd been watching him from a distance for years.

"I don't think we've had the pleasure," said Abeland, brushing himself off and handing over the pistol to the soldier stepping forward for it. He glanced over his shoulder at the inn as the fire consumed it. Richy, Bakon and Egelina-Marie all had rifles trained on them from some of the dozen mounted soldiers.

"Oh, we have, actually," said the red hooded woman. "Mind you, it doesn't matter. I really should thank you, on behalf of your father and all your collective work, for laying all the groundwork for our grand return."

Abeland furrowed his eyebrows. There was something distinct and familiar about her voice. He studied the gold embroidery on the edges of her cloak. "Fair enough, I suppose?"

"Hmm, funny," she replied with sharp disdain. "You know, I was prepared for your antics, though to be honest, I'm surprised you're still doing them at *your* age. Now, to the business of shooting your friends and bringing you for a very public trial. See, I remember how you like an audience."

Audience? thought Abeland. Now he was certain. He waved for her to stop talking, surprising everyone with his audacity. "They're not my friends, and, to be more specific, you wouldn't want to shoot the one you're pointing at."

The woman cocked her head to the side. "Now why would that be?"

Abeland smiled. "Because, Cat, he's your son."

She stared at him in disbelief, she could feel herself losing focus. She glanced at the unshaven man and was ready to give the order to have him shot, when she found she couldn't. "Give me a lantern," she commanded as she dismounted. With lantern in hand, she pushed the night back and studied Bakon's face in detail. After staring at the ground in thought for a while, she turned to Abeland.

"I don't believe you."

Chewing on his lip to hide his satisfaction at confirming her identity, Abeland shrugged. He wondered how she could possibly be alive, and if somehow his brother Lennart was also alive. It seemed like only yesterday that the message had arrived with news of Lennart, Catherine and their three boys' deaths. "Then shoot him. Go on, shoot your long lost son Beldon and be done with it," he said, forcing himself to stand straight. He watched out of the corner of his eye as the ripple of confusion spread from one soldier to the next. The whispers of rumor quickly followed.

She stared at Bakon, looking at his build as much as his face.

"By the way, do you go by the Lady in Red, Duchess Catherine or Caterina Maurice? So many options, and to be honest, I like to be really clear about people's names. I'm a bit obsessive about it," said Abeland. He hoped that after all the years, her ruthless father's decision to change her name when married was still a sore point. Gaston Maurice had been a particularly cold and scheming man.

"Given we're old friends and you'll hang soon, Regent Caterina," she answered sharply.

Abeland blinked in surprise. *Regent?*

Caterina pulled back her hood, revealing her blotchy, heart-shaped face, and a scar that went from her left eye to her chin.

"Oh, you've changed," said Abeland. "More menacing. It's like all your anger and disappointment is trying to break free through that scar."

She struck him in the mouth.

He rubbed his jaw. "Fair enough."

Staring at Bakon, Caterina asked him, "What's your name?"

Bakon swallowed uncomfortably, not sure exactly what games were being played or how the Lady in Red and Abeland knew each other. He glanced at Abeland, wondering how he intended for all of this to play out, or if he had any plan at all. He looked back at the woman. There was something vaguely familiar about her face and her name. With a steady breath, he squeezed Egelina-Marie's hand and answered, "Bakon Cochon."

Caterina raised the lantern again. This time illuminating the grey streaks in her otherwise dark hair. Her green eyes were menacing and feline.

Richy's eyes went wide as he saw the family resemblance. "Woo... you *are* his mother, aren't you?"

Egelina-Marie squeezed Bakon's sweaty hand.

Caterina turned to Egelina-Marie. The intensity of the woman's gaze was nothing like Eg had felt before. "Are you his wife?"

"I'm... I'm his girlfriend," she replied, nervously.

"Is there anything of note on his back?"

Egelina's eyes darted around. "Ah..." She looked at

Bakon trying to remember.

"Don't look at him, look at me," commanded Caterina.

Eg's memory was a locked vault until she saw the hope hidden deep in the woman's eyes. Relaxing, she remembered. "You mean the birthmark on his shoulder, right? It's... ah... it's about the size of a small coin. It's shaped like a... crescent."

Caterina stepped forward and, with her thumb and forefinger, rubbed one of Bakon's earlobes. Both she and Bakon immediately knew. Her cheeks went red and her eyes darted away.

"He's gone!" yelled one of the soldiers. "Abeland Pieman's gone."

"Hunt him down, *now!*" commanded Caterina. She was furious at herself for having taken her attention off one of the few people remaining who could upset her plans. She gestured to Richy. "Hand him over to the local authorities, I have no need of him."

"No!" said Bakon, a pistol immediately making him stop in his tracks as he moved to protect his young friend.

"I'll be okay," said Richy to Bakon. He didn't mean it, and Bakon knew it.

Egelina-Marie gave Richy's arm a squeeze. "We'll see you soon. I promise."

"When pigs fly," said the soldier hauling Richy away.

Caterina leaned into Bakon. "Understand this:

Nothing will derail me from my plans. If you die here, it will be a curious drop in the river of history, nothing more." She rubbed her thumb and forefinger together, and there was no doubt in her mind. Somehow, her little Bel was standing right there, before her. She hadn't felt so rattled in a long, long time.

Twenty years ago, in the snow-covered Republic of Ahemia, six-year-old Beldon accompanied his mother to the signal spire of the castle. He was worried about her. Her feet were dragging, her shoulders slumped, her words had a heaviness to them lately. He hoped holding her hand somehow made things better.

"Duchess Catherine," said the weather Conventioneer she'd summoned.

Caterina winced as she always did at that name. "Thank you for coming. What news do you have of the snow? Will we see a break in the next few days?"

The old conventioneer lowered his eyes, his large white mustache and bushy eyebrows hiding most of his features. "Regretfully, I must to say no. The stories from the farms align with our best instruments, which all point to more snow of this magnitude falling for several weeks yet. My apologies, duchess."

Caterina forced a smile and thanked the old man. She wandered the corridors aimlessly until she came upon Beldon, his beaming little face lifting her shoulders.

"Mama, where are you going?" he asked, tilting his

head preciously.

With a sigh, she replied, "I have to go to see the signal master."

"Can I come?" he asked. She could see in his eyes that it was past his bedtime. He took her hand. "Please?"

"Okay. You know it's a lot of stairs, though?"

"I know, Mama," he replied, setting off in the direction of the signal master's tower.

She'd spent weeks planning and preparing for her husband's surprise birthday party. It had been Beldon's idea, his hope to bring his parents closer together. Now, she'd have to cancel it. With each step, everything seemed colder, lonelier.

Lennart and Caterina had been arguing, loudly, for months. They'd lost their ability to stop when the boys were around. When Beldon asked, as he sometimes did, what it was about, neither of them felt like explaining it. Part of it was rooted in the ambitions of their respective fathers, Marcus Pieman and Gaston Maurice, and part of it was because neither of them knew how to bridge the ever growing gulf between them.

As Caterina knocked on the signal master's bedroom door, she gazed down at little Beldon, who was still holding her hand dearly. "I love you Bel. You know that, right?"

He smiled up at her. "Yes, Mama. I know. I love you, too. Oink!" he said, scrunching his face up.

She smiled back, tapping his nose. "Oink."

"Can we play little piggies when I get to bed?" he asked. "I know it's late already. And it's okay if you say no."

"Well, Bel," she said, drawing out her words. "I don't know…"

"I already got Skells and Bore ready for bed," he offered, his face filled with hope.

She wondered when he'd be old enough to notice when he mispronounced Selvin's name. Half the time he seemed to get it right. She didn't want it to go too soon.

Just as the door started to creak open, she gave Bel a confirming nod. A blurry eyed signal master squinted at the duchess and the little master. "Is there something you need at this hour, my lady?" he asked, rubbing his wrinkly, tired face.

"Sorry to disturb you at this *still* most reasonable hour, but I need you to announce that the party for Duke Lennart is canceled on account of snow."

He scratched his stubbly face. "You know I cannot—"

"Give the reason why, yes, I know. Just get it done," she snapped.

With his instructions understood, the door closed. Caterina and Beldon started their descent down the spiral staircase.

"Mama?" asked Beldon sweetly.

She was in her own little world. The signal master had

reminded her that everything seemed to be a struggle lately. It only made matters worse that she'd been getting letters about her father's heavy-handed attempts at rallying some of the smaller Fare factions under him against the Piemans. The letters were either filled with pleas for her to do something about him, or telling her how they would prefer to follow her, both of which were a joke. She had no influence over Gaston Maurice, and had no proven ability to lead.

Her marriage to Lennart Pieman had been her father's *brilliant* idea, a means to unify the Piemans with the rogue Fare factions he'd gathered at the time. It hadn't worked. She'd been a pawn then, and felt like one now. A few months ago, two of the Fare faction leaders had shown up out of the blue. Lennart had been home, and their presence had taken an open secret and cast it into the light. In the ensuing epic argument, she'd revealed her distain for the Piemans and their vision of the world, and in the heat of the moment, she'd told her husband she couldn't respect him because of it. Everything had gone down hill rapidly from there.

"Mama? Can Skells, Bore and me use the big ballroom to play since there's no party anymore?"

"*Sels or Selvin!*" she snapped. "His name is *Selvin*, and it's Selvin, Bore and *I.*" She was immediately wracked with guilt for snapping at him. It was a horrible habit she had, a defense mechanism she'd developed against her older sisters, designed to throw them off balance. It worked on Lennart particularly well. She glanced down at Beldon's tear filled eyes, the look of having disappointed her on his face. She let go of his hand and sat down on a stair. With her head in her hands, she stared at the cold stone steps. She couldn't look at him, not until she knew he'd forgiven her. "I'm sorry, Belly. I shouldn't have done that. Mama's very sorry."

Beldon looked at her tears as they splashed down, confused and worried. "Someone might see you, Mama," he said of her sitting on a step. She'd never done anything so common before. She had rules about such things, rules she'd told him a hundred times. "Mama, get up."

"I can't right now, Belly. I just can't." Her voice was fragile. "I'm sorry, Bel. I'm so sorry about everything," she said, breaking down.

Bel wrapped his little six-year-old arms around her. "Mama, it's okay. I know you love me. But, Mama, you shouldn't be sitting. Someone might see you," he said, trying to lift her up.

She chuckled at the sweet efforts of her little hero and patted the empty spot beside her. After some hesitation and a glance around, he sat down. "I don't care if someone sees me, Bel. This is the true me. For so long I have been pushed and shoved into a life and destiny I never wanted." She wrapped her arms around him and gave him a kiss on his messy top of dark-blond hair. "I love you. You and Selvin and Boris, all of you. You know that, right?"

"I know, Mama." He hugged her. "Are you worried about something?" he asked astutely.

She rubbed his ear-lobe with her thumb and forefinger as she often did. It reminded her of how soft he'd been as a baby. "I am, a little. There are a lot of things going on." She brushed the hair from his forehead and looked at his gentle eyes. "You're so strong, Bel. You'll always be there for your brothers, right? Always take care of them?"

"Always, Mama," he said proudly, his chin raised.

CHAPTER THREE
LOST WOLF

LeLoup blinked hard and glanced about, rubbing the side of his head where Tee had pistol-whipped him. She was nowhere to be found, though he was certain she was nearby.

The forest leaves rustled as he scurried over to his two henchmen and shook them awake.

He pointed at the unconscious fifteen-year-old. "Take the Watt boy. We're heading back to the horses."

LeLoup felt a buzzing in his head as he surveyed the clearing. The plan had been brilliant. He'd had a traitor within Tee's inner-circle, and yet she'd gotten the better of him. Not only had she made him look like a fool once again, she'd taken a piece of his soul this time. He shook as he remembered the look in her eyes after he'd accidentally shot Elly.

He stared at Elly, a bleeding mess of red and yellow. He glanced around nervously. "Where did you go, Tee?" he wondered, scratching his face furiously. "Are you going to leap out at me? Or have you broken and fled?"

As he went through the possibilities, his heart pounded harder and harder. "What have I done? Why won't this stop?" The buzzing in his head seemed more like arguing voices now. He slapped his own face to silence them.

Just as he was about to leave, he caught a glimpse of the Liar. His custom made triple-barreled, repeating pistol was a work of art, and it had betrayed him. In the moment where he was ready to use the secret, extra bullet, that which gave the pistol its very name, the gun had jammed. He froze, his eyes darting about. With a shaking hand, he snatched the Liar and hurried off, certain he could hear Tee approaching.

Arriving at their horses, LeLoup paced back and forth. His angry, nonsensical mumblings and rantings had become more intense as he'd trekked through the forest. "She's taken my wolf. I need it back. I need it back," he said to the air. Tee's enraged eyes haunted him. The argument inside his head were growing more intense.

"Hey!" yelled Stefano, snapping his fingers to get LeLoup's attention. "Look, I know you're the boss and everything, but you're not making any sense, and you're not listening to us. Frankly, we're getting sick of it. Are we going somewhere with the knocked out twitchy kid, or not? Because if your plan is to do the crazy walk-and-talk all day, then we're out of here."

"Shut up!" yelled LeLoup, whipping out the Liar and pointing it squarely at his henchman.

"Woo there," said Ruffo, the other henchman. "Just calm down, LeLoup."

"LeLoup? Who's that? Is that you? No, it's me," LeLoup muttered to himself, glancing about before settling back on Ruffo.

Stefano rubbed his face in frustration and glanced at Ruffo with a look of disbelief. "What do you want us to do?"

LeLoup smoothed his hair and straightened his dirtied grey suit jacket. "I'm going back after Tee. You two continue on to the inn with the Watt boy. I'll be there soon. I need to get my wolf back."

It hadn't taken LeLoup long to find the trail left by Tee's makeshift stretcher. After following them for a few minutes, and knowing the area well, he took a direct route for the road. Exiting the forest and stepping on to the dirt road, he scanned about. A hundred yards away, he saw a horse and cart stopped. Hugging the forest's edge, he quickly and quietly approached.

The greasy looking driver pushed up his three-point hat with a finger as thick as a sausage. He leaned forward, resting an arm partially on his big belly. His face had several days of grey and black stubble.

He smiled down on the exhausted, dirty, but still pretty girl before him. "That's a nice piece of metal you have there," he said of the shock-stick Tee had pulled out. "Now, why don't you put it down and come keep me company up here? You want me to help your friend, don't you?"

LeLoup listened as he crept ever closer. It was odd seeing Tee without her yellow cloak. She was in a blood and dirt-stained sleeveless blouse, her hair a tangled black mess. Her shock-stick hand was shaking; not in fear, but in fury.

Tee growled. "I *need* your horse and cart!" she yelled, leaping forward.

Time seemed to slow for LeLoup as he caught the look in Tee's eyes. His blood ran cold. All the voices inside him screamed as one.

Two shots rang out, startling Tee and making her slip off the edge of the cart. She fell to the ground, landing on her back and elbows. She stared in complete shock at LeLoup, who was standing only a few yards away, his triple-barreled pistol held high in the air.

"You can't do this!" LeLoup yelled at her, his arm and head shaking. "You can't, that would make you forever the wolf. I need it back. This is not you."

The driver glanced back and forth between Tee and LeLoup. "Who the yig are you? What's he talking about?" he asked her, slowly reaching underneath his seat.

LeLoup flashed a twisted smile at the driver. "Monsieur, I might not sound my best, but please, do not test me. Leave the weapon where it is."

"I don't know what you're talking about," stammered

the driver, leaving his hands low.

LeLoup took careful aim at the man's chest. "Well, I *can* educate you, if you'd like."

None of this made sense to Tee. Seeing LeLoup drained her of the last of her strength. Her body sagged as exhaustion took hold. In a voice laced with defeat, Tee said, "Just kill me already."

"What? No," said LeLoup, staring at her. Inside, he was surprised at his answer. Wasn't this what he'd set out to do? He'd told his henchmen he was going to kill her, didn't he? He glared at the driver, sending a shiver down the man's spine. "Now, Monsieur, *out* of the cart. *Please*."

The driver put his hands up. "Look, let's start over. I don't know who you are, but I'm just trying to help the little lady. She was coming up and—"

LeLoup laughed. "Do you really think you were about to have your way with her? You're an idiot and grossly underestimate her, as have I many times. She'd have beaten you to within a kiss of your last breath."

"I hardly think a little girl—"

"Ah, Monsieur, you are indeed glorious idiot. But, where are my manners? I'm—" and nothing else came out of LeLoup's mouth. His eyes darted around before landing on Tee.

She frowned and stood up slowly. "He's... Andre LeLoup," she said, her expression of one of complete bewilderment. "He... He's the one that shot my friend...

the friend who is *dying* right here." Tee growled, the fury returning to her eyes.

"Wait," pleaded LeLoup, speaking to her rage. "No, back. Go back in!"

The driver looked at Tee and then LeLoup again. "You can talk with the crazy man, I'm going."

Tee glanced at Elly. "If I don't get her to Costello soon, she'll die! Please."

"Costello…" repeated LeLoup, dropping his pistol arm as he suddenly remembered his conversation with Franklin. He'd momentarily forgotten about the Watt boy and his henchmen. He gazed about, and was wondering which direction they were in when the cart driver whipped out a flintlock rifle from under his seat.

LeLoup spun and shot over the man's shoulder, the wind slapping him in the face. "Now, please, if you would be *so kind*," he said, showing his teeth, "clean your little mess that I see piddling off the bench seat, and take yourself for a walk. I hear exercise is good, particularly for those of such blessed girth."

After wiping the bench seat and cart floor with a rag, the man hurried off in the direction he'd come from.

Putting the Liar away, LeLoup approached Tee slowly. She stared at him, confused.

"Tell me how best to help you get… Elly… into the cart," he said, his hands shaking.

Elly stared lazily at the painting on the ceiling as she enjoyed the sounds of an angelic choir. Morning light poured in through two large, open windows. The red and gold curtains had been drawn aside, probably by the monk that had been keeping an eye on her.

Before she could really wonder about where the monk had ventured off to, she heard it—Tee's distinctive footfalls, blazing a trail down the marble corridors. Excitement built in Elly until finally she saw Tee burst through the doorway. For a moment, Tee was a blur of red, until Elly could see she was in the red and gold colors of the abbey.

For all of their thirteen years, they'd been best friends. Before they'd been able to talk or walk, they'd had each other. They had overcome everything together, including the secrets that had most recently threatened to tear them apart, along with Franklin's betrayal. When LeLoup had shot her, Elly's greatest fear had been what would happen to Tee if she died.

Elly winced in pain as she tried to sit up and failed. Tee leapt to Elly's low bedside and buried her head beside Elly, her long black hair everywhere. Tee wrapped her arms around Elly, and with a choked up voice asked, "How... ah... how are you feeling?"

"I'm okay," replied Elly weakly. "Good thing we have the no dying rule, right?"

"Yeah," replied Tee, crying.

Elly carefully wrapped her arms around Tee, pushing through the pain. "You saved me. We're okay now." Tee hugged Elly harder, her body shaking. Elly couldn't understand her incoherent mumbles, but there was a weight and pain in her voice that she didn't recognize. "I'm okay, you saved me," Elly kept repeating. As the seconds passed, her anxiety crept up. "Tee? Are we okay?"

Elly felt her gaze pulled to the doorway. Slowly, a mysterious form stepped into the room. Her blood ran cold as she recognized LeLoup. When she'd last seen him, at the other end of his triple-barreled pistol just before he'd shot her, he'd looked different. His hair was now a mess, his face unshaven, and his grey suit was dirty and stained. His pistol was strapped to his leg, but hung there as if he had no idea it existed.

As he turned, Elly saw the once piercing green eyes were now emerald windows to a shattered soul. He was a man undone. A strange smile crossed his lips as he and Elly made eye contact. "It is… good to see you are alive," he said, his voice was oddly hesitant. His eyes darted away, bouncing around the room before settling on the window. "Elly… You must fix Tee. She's taken my wolf, but she's using it. I can't get it back until she's fixed. I need it back, because without it, who am I?" He rubbed his cheek, confused. "Who am I?"

Elly felt Tee tense. "Tee, is he insane?"

Tee turned and glared at LeLoup.

LeLoup recoiled at her gaze. "No! *No!* Give me back my wolf! Please, don't eat me. Please!" He covered his face and looked out the window again. "You need to get well, and then I will take it back. You can't keep it."

Elly saw the fragile look in Tee's eyes and nodded. She couldn't imagine what had happened—why he was there, why Tee had that look—but Elly knew it was now her turn to be the defender. "Go," she said to LeLoup.

"One day I will find you, Tee... And... and I will become *me* again," he said, leaving.

CHAPTER FOUR

DA BOSS

The tea cup took off out of Franklin's grip and smashed on the wall. "YIG!" he cursed, glaring at the fading spasm in his hand. They'd been coming and going ever since Tee had shocked him, and were strong enough to shake him awake in the night. Every spasm added fuel to his fiery temperament.

"That's four cups, kid. You're getting expensive," said Stefano, annoyed, rubbing his dark, stubbly face. The henchman's arms and neck were as thick as they were hairy. "Don't throw the rest of the breakfast, okay? I'm still working on it."

Franklin glared at the newly shattered cup through his long blond bangs, which hid the black eye from Elly. He turned from the plate of dry toast, the plate of sausage, and finally to the tea pot. No matter how many cups he destroyed, the pot wouldn't care.

"Hey, hands off the pot," said Stefano, knocking Franklin's hands back. "You were doing that mumbling nonsense thing again, kid. I heard you say that girl's name this time. Geez kid, look, she zapped you. She zapped all of us. You'll get better."

"And if I don't?" asked Franklin angrily. "I'm an *inventor*. I need my hands, and no distractions. I can't be flailing about like an idiot. I have every right—"

"Hey!" yelled Stefano, slamming his hand down on the table rattling the dishes. "*You* listen up now, kid. I've had enough of your whining. Suck it up, or put your anger to use, that's what my Ma used to say. The other option is I just snap that neck of yours like a… like a… a twig. Either way, get quiet—and quick."

Franklin was all ready to unleash whatever fury he had in him when he realized that Stefano was right, in his own simplistic way. There was no point seething with anger and twisting himself up more and more, especially when there was no Tee around to direct it at.

Stefano pointed with his thumb at the tea stains. "You better hope that LeLoup shows up, because let me tell you, Franky, Ruffo and I, we ain't paying for jack."

Franklin frowned. "Does jack mean nothing? Did you just imply you were going to pay for *everything?*"

Stefano's fists made a noise like tightening leather just as Ruffo walked in. He was bigger than Stefano. His face was clean shaven and his shoulder length brown-red hair was a wet mess. Like Franklin and Stefano, he was dressed exactly like he was the day before, just more wrinkled. "That crackpot LeLoup here yet?" he asked.

"No," said Stefano, disgusted.

Ruffo cursed, looking at the breakfast. "The guy's not coming back, then." He dropped himself in a chair. It shook as it struggled to hold together under his wall-like frame. "This LeLoup guy, he's missing some cards, you know? What's with this thing he's got for that sixteen-year-old girl? I mean, that's not right."

"Thirteen," corrected Franklin. "She's thirteen."

"Geez, really?" asked Ruffo, smoothing his hair.

"I am *dead* certain," replied Franklin, rubbing the black eye Elly had given him.

Ruffo rubbed his face in embarrassment. "We got our butts kicked by a thirteen-year-old girl? Man, she's got a lot of anger and skill for a kid, but still." He drummed his fingers on the table for a few seconds. "Okay, the official story, though, if any word of this gets out, she was sixteen."

"Eighteen," offered Stefano.

"Yeah, eighteen," replied Ruffo. "That's better."

"Yeah, and there were three of her," proposed Franklin with a half-smile.

Stefano nudged him with a laugh. "Hey, someone's getting it."

Franklin spread his fingers flat and wide on the table. He stared at them while the two thugs continued their banter. Finally, he interrupted them. "So, am I your prisoner or not? We have to assume that LeLoup's not coming back, so—"

"Hey, quiet," said Stefano, smacking Franklin in the chest, nearly knocking him clean over. "If the innkeeper hears that, she's going to come after us."

"You guys can take her," said Franklin, trying *not* to look like Stefano had just knocked the wind out of him, which he had.

Ruffo leaned across the table. "That's not the point, Franky. Do you know why we're in here without paying upfront? Because this lady knows who we are, and she's got friends that are ten times scarier than us or LeLoup. Heck, she's *twenty* times scarier than us. We do wrong by her, or make her go missing, we're looking over our shoulders for the rest of our lives. And that's if we're lucky."

Franklin glanced at Stefano and was surprised to see the same expression of serious concern. "Really? I wouldn't have guessed that. I mean, she's a petite lady, who's what, fifty? Sixty? Renee doesn't sound like a big tough name to me."

Stefano leaned in. "I heard she used to run the Carvalho gang years ago."

"Were they with the Fare or Tub?" asked Franklin.

"The who?" asked Stefano, confused. He looked at Ruffo. "Tubs? I'm trying to educate the kid and he's talking to me about bathing?"

Franklin rubbed the bridge of his nose as he recalled

that the Tub and Fare were called secret societies for a reason. He gestured for Stefano to continue.

"The Carvalhos used to run things, unofficial like, in the northern part of Farkees. This lady, Renee—I heard she started as a slave in Kaban, and somehow made her way up. Did some nasty evil stuff on the way, and no one, let me tell you, *no one* messes with that old lady."

Franklin couldn't believe how impressed the guys seemed. "Well, that sounds—"

Ruffo cut him off with a gesture. "It's scary, that's what it is, Franky. Now she runs this place. I don't know why, but I ain't asking. Maybe she wanted a change of scenery, maybe she's been exiled. Maybe she just up and retired."

Rocking his chair on its back legs, Franklin flipped his gaze between the two guys. He kept expecting them to finally crack and admit they were joking, but so far, he couldn't detect anything. "So a little lady like that could run some big... what did you call it, gang? Is that like an army?"

"Yeah, I suppose," said Ruffo, scratching his head. "Don't judge her by the way she looks at first glance. Nah, this lady, she's an example of you got to look at what's on the inside. She's got brains."

"Determination and ruthlessness, too," added Stefano. "Without those, she'd have snapped like a... a..."

"A twig?" offered Franklin.

"Yeah," said Stefano, sitting back. "Like a twig."

Franklin mulled over what they were saying. "When the Yellow Hoods and I fought the Red Hoods and some soldiers, I saw much of the same thing, I guess. I also saw how elementary fighting was, how it was simply about timing and basic anatomy. Hit someone when they were ready for it? It had no effect. But even a small fist from a child like Mounira, at the right moment in the right place? You could go down like a sack of—"

"Twigs," interjected Stefano.

"Ah… sure," replied Franklin.

Ruffo scoffed. "Fighting is a lot of things, but it's not easy or about brainy stuff like that. It's about hitting a man where it counts, hard" said Ruffo.

"Or shooting him," offered Stefano.

Ruffo gestured that the point was a good one and took another bite of salty sausage.

"I bet I could take you down," said Franklin squarely to Ruffo. "I bet I could take you down with a single hit." He kept his sweaty hands below the table, out of sight.

Ruffo laughed, nearly spitting out his mouthful of breakfast. "No way."

Franklin licked the side of his mouth, his eyes moving between the two men. Leaning forward, he said, "If I do, you guys listen to my plan. Just *listen* to it. If you like it, you follow *me*."

"We're going to listen to some punk kid? Why would

we do that?" asked Stefano.

"It'll never happen," said Ruffo, laughing.

"I know, I know—but still, why would we do that?" he asked, crossing his arms and glaring at Franklin. "Come on, kid, tell me why."

"Because I have a plan, and, much like Renee, *I'm* a lot scarier on the inside than *I* look," replied Franklin.

"Ha," said Stefano.

Just as Ruffo stood and gestured for Franklin to take his best shot, Franklin leaped forward and hit him in the ear for all that he was worth. Ruffo went down immediately.

Stefano grabbed Franklin with one hand and put a knife to his throat. "What the yig did you do?" he said, glancing over his shoulder. "Ruffo, you okay?"

Ruffo groaned in response, and then a hand showed up on the table, followed eventually by the top of Ruffo's head. "What'd you do, you little pargo? My world's spinning," he said, his words coming out slowly.

Franklin grinned proudly. He'd risked everything and it had worked, at least so far. He felt compelled to show them just how smart he was. "I noticed that you were wincing every now and then, moving your head to the right. That meant you had a nasty ear infection. So I—"

"You slammed me," interrupted Ruffo, carefully crawling back into his chair. "Yeah, I get it. Let him go, Stefano. Let's hear what the *genius* has to say. Maybe he's not as dumb as he looks."

"By the way, I have an idea how to fix that ear," offered Franklin, realizing his position with the two thugs wasn't yet secure.

"What's this plan of yours?" asked Ruffo.

Franklin interlocked his fingers and leaned forward, his head down. He let a few seconds pass to build up the moment. He then looked at them and smiled. "We don't really need LeLoup to do his plan, now do we?"

CHAPTER FIVE
DEATH OF THE HOUND

The early evening light felt harsh to Gretel as she attempted to open her eyes. Slowly sitting up, she saw the Hound sitting on the grass ten feet away, lost in thought facing the downing sun. He was wearing clothes she didn't recognize.

For a while she watched him and the sun. She asked softly, "What are you thinking about?"

"Where we go from here," he replied, standing and coming to sit beside her. "How are you feeling?"

Gretel sat up slowly. "Better. I'm a bit hungry and thirsty."

"That's good," he said. "I was worried you weren't going to ever wake up." He stepped away and then returned with some bread and a wineskin. "It's filled with water."

"I can't believe it's already the end of the day," said Gretel, taking a drink from the wineskin.

"It's been two days," answered the Hound.

Gretel was surprised. "Is that why you have those clothes?"

He glanced down at them. "I didn't steal them. I was tempted to, but... you made me feel like that would be wrong. I mean, I know it's kind of wrong in my head, but that hasn't stopped me in a long, long time.

"The route near here is really bumpy. The first merchant paid me with these clothes, the other two in bits of food and water. I also got that blanket you're wrapped in," he said, pointing awkwardly.

"Oh," she replied. She liked how he had an air of polite distance, a shyness that was in sharp contrast to his brutish appearance and her first impressions of him. "How are you feeling?"

He rolled up a cream colored sleeve and stared at the scarred arm underneath. "I can't feel much. It's... going to take some getting used to. Touch my arm, tell me how it is."

Hesitantly, Gretel reached over and gently put her hand on his arm. The skin was hot and rough. She moved her fingers along the scar ridges, each feeling like the small stone mountain of pain. "Can you feel any of that?"

"A little," he said, taking his arm back.

She crossed her legs. "The woman who sold me the salves told me that the feeling should return, in time."

"I hope so, but maybe she was just trying to sell you

more salves," he said. "Sorry, I don't mean to be cynical. If it doesn't, I'll live." With an awkward swallow, he turned and looked into her light brown eyes. "I need to know something. Why did you save me? You stole from Hans to pay for salves. You nearly got killed. Why save me? I'm nobody."

Gretel thought back to that moment when they found him, bloody and burned with wreckage all about. "Did you want to die?" she asked, not ready to hear the answer.

"I don't know. I just remember wanting the pain to stop."

She looked into eyes that had once harbored so much pain and anguish, but were now home to tender confusion. "You came to our home and ended Mother's reign of terror. You humbled Hans, something I never thought possible. Then when I saw you lying there, broken and beaten, cold and scared, I felt something strange. I wasn't sickened, as I expected, but... I don't know, I felt connected to you... like I could be whole, somehow, with you."

The Hound nodded, absorbing what she'd said but not sure what to make of it. He broke off a piece of bread and handed it to her. "When you were asleep, you kept talking about the Yellow Hood. Sometimes you called her the Yellow Fury, sometimes the Yellow Sorrow." He shifted uncomfortably, not sure he should even be talking about the subject. "That's the girl who went crazy after you killed that guy on the horse, right?"

Gretel's face went pale, her eyes lowered.

For a while, they sat in silence watching the diminishing brilliance of the sunset.

With an awkward sigh, Gretel answered, "The Ginger is a strange thing. It was as if during the battle with the Yellow Hoods, it lost its grip on me. I remember the sick joy of killing that man and seeing her erupt. But then she looked at me, and I felt horror and regret for what I'd done. It was in that moment that I became *me* again. I was instantly ashamed of who I'd been." She stared at the ground.

"I understand," said the Hound. "I have many layers of shame, many lives I've walked away from in hopes of finding a new one that would let me be better than the last. Each one seemed to be worse than the one before it."

Gretel took his hand. "I hate that feeling. When I was taking care of you, I felt like all of that didn't matter."

"You helped me. You're a good person," he offered.

"Am I? Does one good act clean the slate? I don't trust myself," she said. "I don't know who I am."

The Hound hung his head. "I hope it means something. It's got to."

They watched the sun bury itself below the horizon.

Gretel wondered if he could feel her hand in his. Despite his wounds and strange tufts of sprouting hair in his otherwise bald face, he was beautiful to her. "What's your name?"

"The Hound," he replied without thinking.

"No, your real name," she pressed.

He glanced at her, then back at the sky. "It's The Hound."

She was about to push harder when a silly thought popped to mind. "Well, if you're going to be like that, then you have to call me Regretel."

He laughed, surprising himself. Turning to her, he saw the image that he'd focused on to fight the pain. The face that never failed to light up his soul. The fifteen year difference between them felt like he'd simply taken longer to get to a worthy point in his life.

"You had a name once. What was it?" she asked gently.

He stared at her, unsure of himself. "I've gone by a lot of names, had a lot of different lives. But my first name... was Raymond."

Gretel rubbed her nose and sniffled. "I like that name."

The Hound shrugged. "I don't remember the guy."

"Well, you aren't the Hound anymore. He died in that crash. He was hairy, and chained to whoever made those shocking gloves. You have no master anymore, you are nobody's lapdog," said Gretel, thinking. "How about Ray?"

He frowned at her. "Why would I call myself that?"

"Because you give me hope. You're my Ray of Hope."

He frowned even more. "I don't know if I like that. I've never cared for word jokes."

"You liked Regretel," she pointed out.

He laughed. "Yeah. I guess so. Maybe the Hound is dead."

She smiled. "I've decided. You're Ray. Can you live with it?"

"I think so."

Reaching over, he pulled a two foot long darkly wrapped item into his lap. "Do you want to talk about what happened?" he asked, knowing he was killing the mood but wanting to get it off his chest. "Or do we leave the past in the past?"

She stared at the ground, and nodded nervously.

He removed the cloth wrapping, revealing Hans' broken rapier. "I didn't kill him. I was tempted, though. I honestly didn't know how you'd feel about it, so I left him severely injured. I think I broke his arm, maybe his leg, too."

Gretel glanced at him and then at the rapier. Unconsciously she started rocking herself back and forth.

"After he was down and no threat, I picked this and you up and went back to the cabin to check on Saul. He was gone. Not sure what to do, I just started walking. If you don't want this, I'll—"

Gretel stood and threw the rapier as far as she could.

Ray caught her as she stumbled backwards.

"That felt good," she said, laughing.

"What now?" he asked, steadying her on her own two feet.

"In the morning, we start our road to redemption."

CHAPTER SIX
PIECES OF THE PIEMAN

Abeland groped around for something to cover his head and block the morning sun. The bed he'd cobbled together from the remains of Richelle's estate had included a mattress and makeshift pillow, but no blanket. He sat up and yawned, gazing through the broken glass window. The fresh, warm summer air felt good. "Might as well get another breathing treatment in before breakfast," he said, getting up and reaching for his shirt.

It had been a challenging couple of days to shake all of his pursuers, but once he had, he'd made his way to Richelle's in hopes of meeting up with her. Along the way, he heard of the Laros coup, the dissolving of its parliament and the hunt for Richelle. He was relieved that there was no word of her having been captured or killed.

He nodded at the broom leaning against the far wall. It had been a long, long time since he'd used one, but it had felt right bringing a bit of order to the master bedroom before sleeping in it. It was one way of reclaiming the mob-ravaged home of his niece. Picking up the broom, he headed for the basement and the secret entrance to the laboratory where his spare breathing apparatus was set up.

As he double checked the dials and levers of his machine, he noticed a subtle closet door. Walking over and opening it, he laughed and clapped his hands. Richelle had several of his old shirts, pants and even one of his tricked-out long coats. "You are simply the best niece, ever," he said. "The sun won't set today until I figure out what happened to you, I promise."

With the knobs properly calibrated and a fresh dose of medicine in place, Abeland sat in the chair and pulled down the barbaric looking helmet. For the next hour, as his lungs were exercised and the medicine pushed in, he planned his day.

After washing and dressing in fresh clothes, Abeland found a renewed sense of daring. He went into the small village nearby and bought some fruit, bread and meat for the day with coins from Richelle's secret cache. No one recognized him, even all dressed up. Maybe it was the lack of his customary eyepatch or monocle. Maybe it was because no one was looking for Piemans. Either way, he knew not to push his luck.

He set his sack of goods on the kitchen table and put the lone surviving plate down gently. The white porcelain plate had a crack running from the edge through the

Pieman's crest. He remembered seeing a plate like that at Lennart's, the last time he'd dropped in to visit. He'd played with little Beldon, and then, as always, he'd argued with his brother about spies and plots and things that they seemed to violently agree on rather than disagree about. He vowed to do right by his brother and make sure that his son would have a good life.

Abeland pushed the cracked plate away and rubbed his forehead. He'd lost his appetite. It was rare that he let his mind wander out of bounds, and always felt uneasy when it returned.

He gazed out a broken kitchen window at the beautiful day. He wondered how disciplined Caterina was, and how she would handle discovering that her little boy Beldon was now *Bakon*, alive and well. He was all but certain she wouldn't be distracted for long, one way or the other. His sense of family responsibility was confused. Should he be trying to rescue Bakon because he was a Pieman, or treat him like a Maurice? He was Richelle's brother, but neither of them knew that, which made it seem less real.

Walking out into the garden, he pondered his next move. Richelle was out there, somewhere. He needed to reach out to his spy network to find her, but if he tried too hard, he was sure that Caterina would hear of it. He had to be smart and careful, the latter of which he rarely was, particularly when he was by himself.

Returning inside and climbing the stairs to the second

floor, Abeland started feeling along the trim of the corridor and of every room, looking for a secret panel. It was standard practice for the Piemans to hide their real offices, unless they were in Teuton. He doubted Richelle would have broken with tradition. He'd already searched the basement to no avail.

"Turn around!" boomed a voice from the bottom of the staircase.

Abeland clutched his chest. "You scared the ghost out of me," he said chuckling. "I'm glad to see you're not dead."

"We Piemans *are* hard to kill," replied Richelle, relieved to see her uncle.

"We are, indeed," he said, trotting down the stairs.

Richelle gave him a big hug. "Is that red in your cheeks, uncle? Is emotion creeping in along with the grey?" she asked.

"What? Never," he said, touching his hair. "Have you perchance been taken to a new fashion in my absence?" She resembled a drowned cat who had then gone through a windstorm. Her hair was twisted and knotted, her clothes filthy and ruined. She had dried blood on her face and hands.

Richelle pulled a twig out of her hair. "I took a flying leap off a rail-raft into a lake. The hundred yard drop was exhilarating, but the sudden stop was rather painful. It's been a long road home." She gave Abe a smile. "It's good to see you. I thought *you* were dead, and with Opa captured, I thought I was all that was left."

"So father's been captured?"

"Yes, by the Lady in Red," answered Richelle.

Abeland glanced about. "Hmm, so she was striking at us from every angle she could, then. She must have a lot of royals in her pocket."

"Where have you been?" asked Richelle.

"Prison, betrayed by Simon. I escaped recently and then was nearly captured by her. I then made my way here. So let me ask, is rail-raft jumping a new sport now? From the vanguard of innovation to just... things to do when bored?"

"Did I mention the Fare soldiers trying to kill me?"

"No," replied Abeland. "You left that part out."

Richelle smiled. "It turns out Ron-Paul Silskin is working for Caterina. He lead the ambush. Mister Jenny was there, too, though I think he's the reason I had a chance to escape."

Abeland was surprised. "Jenny, after all this time? Huh. It's like the past is coming back to haunt us."

Richelle detected something as he averted his gaze. "What is it? You're hiding something from me."

He was out of practice at keeping things from her. He'd trained her to notice the little things, and she was doing him proud, as always. "We need to talk for a moment." Over the next ten minutes, he shared with her the discovery that her mother was alive, and that she was the Lady in Red. After that had settled in, he went on to tell her about her three brothers and why he and Marcus had never told her. To his surprise, she wasn't angry

"Once... I think I was about ten, you told me about my brothers. It was one of those rare occasions where you were drunk before lunch. Something was bothering you, and I listened, and then you told me about them and my parents, and how much I meant to you. I didn't know if you were telling the truth so I went to Opa. He took me into his secret office and sat me down. He gave me a cookie and told me everything. I was angry for months. But that was then. I'm not going to let old anger haunt or control me. That woman isn't my mother, she's just the woman who birthed me." Her hands shook, betraying her air of calm.

He nodded, stopping himself from consoling her; it had never been his role. He'd always been the one to pick her up, set her focus and run with her, not the one to cuddle her in the dark moments. "Shall we put her on the revenge list?"

"The list is *all* her now," replied Richelle.

"So, what do we do next? I have no idea where we stand," admitted Abeland.

Richelle bent down and picked at some chards of an old vase, thinking. "Simon should have the steam engine plans by now."

"It was finally invented, then? Excellent. Klaus, I presume," said Abeland.

"Watt, actually. Yes, I was surprised as well. Anyway, Simon's still using the same manor in Staaten, so we should be okay."

Abeland raised a finger. "A point on that—we'll need to be careful. Besides being the Lady in Red, I think Caterina serves as Regent for Staaten. I noticed an insignia on some of her soldiers."

Richelle nodded. "We should check any messages they're sending by Neumatic Tube."

"Check?" said Abeland, surprised.

"I don't invent much," replied Richelle, "but I did build a way to intercept most messages, at least within a region."

"Clever girl," replied Abeland.

Richelle rolled her eyes. "Girl indeed. Anyway, we should get to my office. Care to lead the way?" she asked gesturing to the stairs.

Looking sheepish, he replied, "Um… why don't you go first? I'll follow your lead."

CHAPTER SEVEN

ONE FOR THE ROAD

The door of the abbey bedroom creaked open, rousing Tee from her troubled sleep. As the soft footsteps came closer, Tee peeked out at the world. When the figure bent down and laid his hand on her back, she knew immediately who it was.

"Dad?" said Tee sitting up and rubbing her eyes.

"Hi, little love," he replied, his voice warm and loving.

She pulled him into a tight hug. "I've missed you so much!"

"I've missed you, too," he said, rocking her gently. "The Abbott tells me you've been through a lot." He remembered leaving a note for Tee, detailing that his wife, Jennifer, and he were going to check out some concerns in Mineau. He'd been certain they would see her for dinner. He was wrong. "Mind if I open the curtains?"

Tee sniffed and wiped her tears. "No, go ahead. What

time is it?"

"Probably about six in the morning," he said as he tied the curtains back. "I got in two hours ago."

"Six, already? I should be doing my workout," she said pulling her blanket aside instinctively. She then looked at him and smiled.

"So you really do take it that seriously, don't you?" he asked, smiling.

Tee nodded.

He glanced about the small room. "This is a nice little room they have you in. Just enough room for the necessities." He gestured to the sparse furniture.

"They gave Elly a visiting bishop's room," said Tee. "I'm not in here much—just to sleep."

William stared at her and shook his head. "How can you look so much older? It's only been a few days."

"It's been weeks," replied Tee, chuckling. "You always do that." Her smile halted as she sensed something from him. "Are you okay, Dad? You look thinner. Tired."

He sat beside her and patted her hand. "I'm doing okay. I came here as quickly as I could, that's all. You did a great job leaving me those coded messages, from Elly's back doorframe with the chalk, to the notes with the innkeepers. I'm so proud of you. You did everything we told you to do in a crisis." He gave her a kiss on the head. "Well done."

A sense of relief washed over Tee. "I kept wondering

if —"

"And you'll never feel that way again. Right?"

Tee nodded.

"So, how are you doing, love?" he asked, brushing her long, black hair out of her face.

She looked at her hands. "Dad, Elly… she almost…"

He took her back into a hug. "Shh. She's doing fine. You did great."

"But I nearly… I nearly…" Tears streamed down her face.

He rocked her. "Nearly doesn't count. It doesn't matter what it was," he said, his magical voice patching up some of the holes in her soul. He smiled as she sighed. "You're becoming a remarkable woman. I'm so proud."

Tee chuckled. "You've said proud about five times."

He laughed. "Your mother has a better vocabulary. She reads more."

"Yeah." Tee wiped her eyes and nose. "Is Mom here?"

Standing up and looking out the window, William kicked himself. He didn't want to talk about what was going on back home. "No. She's helping the people deal with what happened, along with Squeals and Bore. We agreed that I should find you. We were certain you were okay, but still, we worried."

"Dad?" asked Tee, her eyes welling up and chin quivering.

"Yeah?" he replied, rubbing her back.

"Can I... Can I tell you everything? I just feel so heavy," she started to cry.

Without thinking, he reached into a long forgotten pocket and pulled out an old, yellow and brown handkerchief. "Here."

Tee took it and chuckled, her face a mess. "You still have this?" she asked in disbelief. "I made it when I was three."

"It's always been there, it's my lucky handkerchief," he replied. "You made it for one of my burf-days, as you called it back then." He nodded. "I didn't know it was there, until just now. Funny how life is sometimes."

She wiped her face and nodded. She then took the next hour to fill William in on her version of events, from Anna Kundle Maucher's ill-fated plan to take on the Pieman's that resulted in her capture and Pierre de Montagne's death, to LeLoup's help. As her burden lightened, his shoulders drooped and his face became more solemn.

Gazing out the window and holding her hand, he said, "You shouldn't have had to go through all of that. I... don't know what to say."

"I'm stronger for it, right, Dad?"

He turned to her, nodding. "Incredibly so. I'm going to say it again."

"What's that?" asked Tee, confused.

"Proud. I'm so proud of you," he said with a grin.

Tee sighed. She squeezed his hand. "Can we go home now?"

His eyes darted around the room, which had gone from cozy to confining. "No. I'm sorry, Little Love. It's not safe," he said, his voice trembling slightly. "You need to stay with Christina and the others."

"But I can help," said Tee, frowning. She squinted. "What's going on?"

"Everything is fine, and you're amazing, but I can't have you come. Not yet. I need you here," he replied.

"Christina's not even here," said Tee.

"Actually, the Abbott told me Christina and Mounira arrived last night. I'm surprised Mounira hasn't bolted into your room to wake you up." He stared out the window. "Listen, I know Christina can be a bit… intense sometimes, but she's a good person. I'll send word, probably in a month or two, for you, Elly and Mounira to come home."

"Okay," replied Tee reluctantly. "Are you sure Christina won't mind?"

"I'm going to have a talk with her. It'll be okay," he said with an odd smile.

Tee glanced about. "I'd like to go do my exercises now, if that's okay. You're not going to leave without saying goodbye, are you?"

"No way," he said, giving her a kiss. "And you know

what, if you don't mind, I'd like to join you for that workout. Maybe you could show me some of your moves."

"Okay," she replied with a big smile. "I'll meet you in the courtyard in ten minutes."

———⌒———

Elly laid on one of the abbey's courtyard benches, propped up with pillows. The black wooden wheelchair was on one side, a table with the remnants of a breakfast of tea and toast on the other.

She put down her book on the mountain of pillows and gazed at the manicured gardens. The surrounding old-world buildings protected the courtyard's beauty from the rest of the world. She loved the serenity of the abbey in the early morning, and the fireflies at night.

"Do you have need of anything?" asked one of the monks.

"No thanks, Jayne. I am fine, thank you," said Elly with an appreciative smile.

"It is our duty, and our honor," replied the red and gold robed monk. He bowed and left.

Elly glanced around, feeling something was missing. It had been there since she'd arrived that morning, and now it was gone. Then it hit her. She couldn't hear Tee and William sparring any more. She glanced up at the sun, her hand over her eyes. She wasn't very skilled at telling time from the position of the sun, but she knew it wasn't lunch time yet.

"Is everything alright?" asked another monk. "It is nine o'clock and twenty minutes, if you were curious about the time."

"Thank you... Malcolm?"

The monk nodded and left.

Every day had been similar, and though she'd expected to get quickly tired of it, Elly still loved being spoiled. Tee had started teasing her about the extent, which Elly took as a sign that the days of the dark and brooding Tee were going to pass.

"Hello, Elly," said William, walking up and wiping his flushed face with a towel. A monk quickly took it from him and disappeared. "I was just on my way to talk with Christina and noticed you out of the corner of my eye. You're looking comfortable."

She smiled. "Did you manage to keep up with her? I heard the two of you."

He glanced over his shoulder. "She's really good. Honestly, I'm surprised, and exhausted. I don't remember her always being that intense. Is that new?"

"She's just... um..." Elly wasn't sure how to answer and then stopped, noting the look in his eyes didn't align with his question. "Is everything okay, Monsieur Baker?"

"Yes, yes. Well, as much as could be expected, given what's happened, I suppose," he said, offering the classic smile she used to see nearly every day when she'd pop over to Tee's house.

"Are my parents with you?" she asked eagerly.

William gently shook his head. "Your parents are helping Jennifer in Mineau. They're well, and, of course, worried about you." He crouched down and looked at her, eye to eye. "How are you doing? You've been shot, but I've heard you're recovering well."

Elly unconsciously touched her bandaged side. "I'm doing okay. I can move around a bit now, but it still hurts. Yesterday, I made it through without the pain-stopping elixir the monks make. It's made with the poppies from the nearby fields, and while it smells terrible, it tastes worse. But some good came of it—I've discovered chemistry! One of the monks gave me a book he wrote about how they make it. It's fascinating."

"Really? Huh," he said with a laugh. "So, you've discovered something of interest to you?"

Her eyes sparkled. "Apparently, a few of the monks used to be inventors, though they won't call themselves that. They've been giving me every book on the subject, its history, that they can find. I can't wait until I can make my own little lab and try some of my ideas." She chuckled and smiled.

"What is it?" he asked.

Elly tried to sit up, not sure exactly how to put it. "To be honest, I always wished I could be like Tee. The way she would look at things sometimes, the wheels in her head turning. I never thought I was like that, despite what Tee would say. But now, especially with the secrets she shared with me… I feel different. I feel free, and I'm loving it."

"What did Tee tell you?" asked William, his face tensing.

She studied his steely expression. She could sense his concern and figured that Tee hadn't shared what she'd told her. It warmed her heart to know that Tee really was her sister against everything, and nothing would ever be able to come between them again. "She said my real last name is DeBoeuf and I'm related to a leader of the Tub, the one called the Butcher. She also said I'm as much of an Abominator as she is."

"When I was slipping in and out of consciousness, I thought a lot about it. I feel like I've awakened a new person."

William stroked his beard pensively.

She'd never seen him with a look she couldn't read, and it made her reflect on how little she really knew him. "Is my last name really DeBoeuf?" she asked, bracing herself.

After some hesitation, he replied, "It is. How do you feel about that?"

"Excited, confused. I'm not really sure. I trust my parents, and I'm sure they have a very good reason for it."

"They do. We all do," said William with a sigh. "But, look at this pile of books. Are these all about chemistry? Have you read them all?"

"Yes, but I keep them here for when I need to go back for reference. Some of the monks have started teasing me, calling me the River. Apparently there's a Staaten dialect with an expression about a river washing away... all the wood? Or something? I don't remember. Does that make any sense?"

William skimmed through the titles of the books. "Jennifer calls someone like that a ravaging reader. I always imagine someone ripping all the pages out and eating them when she says that," he replied with a chuckle. "This is an impressive list, Elly. You understand all of this?"

"Not all of it, but it's making more and more sense. Sometimes one of the monks is able to explain something to me that I'm stuck on, but for the most part, I'm figuring it out. Like I said, I want to try things soon."

"Just don't blow yourself up, your mother would be really upset," said William with a fake stern look.

"No worries," she replied with a wink. She watched as his expression melted away and he gazed at the main building of the abbey. "Are you worried about Tee?"

"We had a good talk," he said, turning to her. "But still, I am. I'm her father. We always worry about our little girls, even when they grow up to be fearless warriors."

She narrowed her eyes and studied him. "She'll be okay. I won't let anything happen to her. I don't think Mounira will either."

William rubbed his face. "She's carrying a heavy burden."

"It's getting lighter each day," she said, interrupting.

Nodding, he said, "Thank you, Elly. It means a lot that she has a friend like you."

"She's my girl, my sister. Even if she finds a nice Benjamin someday, I'll still be there," she said.

William laughed. "She'll never outlive that first crush. He was a nice boy."

Elly smiled.

"I better catch Christina before she wanders off somewhere. Listen, it was great to see you."

"Wait. We aren't coming with you?" asked Elly confused. "I thought once I heard your voice, that—"

He scratched his nose. "You and Tee... peas in a pod. You need to stay with Christina a while longer. I'll see you in a few months, if not before. Take care, Elly."

"You, too," she replied. She watched suspiciously as he went to the main building, her head shaking unconsciously.

William closed the door to the Abbott's office after Christina entered. It was decorated with the expected trappings of a religious life, from its books, to the small paintings that hung on the walls, to the bust in the corner.

Christina glared at the room, her loathing of organized religion poorly hidden.

"I just ran into Mounira. Where did that mechanical arm come from?" asked William. "I've never seen anything like it."

She sat in one of two old chairs and folded her arms. "Christophe made it for her."

"Very funny," replied William.

Christina's expression hardened. "She said he made it. Do you know her to lie?"

"No one's seen him do anything but stare at walls and mumble in years," replied William.

"And Mounira claims he came to life around her. I spent some time with him when we were there, but he just stayed locked in his head. She couldn't explain it."

William frowned, and sat down. "You're serious?"

"Do I joke?" snapped Christina, pushing her hair back over her ears.

"And you believe her?"

Christina glared at him. "No, I think a one-armed southerner with no history of inventing created a state of the art piece of technology without a single person noticing."

William shook his head. "I see your sarcasm is alive and well," he retorted. He'd always had an awkward relationship with Christina, and her relationship with

Jennifer was worse. They were almost visual opposites, never mind their personalities and beliefs. William had never gotten the whole story, but knew enough to stay out of it.

"You said you needed to talk to me, and you aren't taking them with you. Why?" asked Christina, leaning forward. "I've done my part, and more."

He stared at the floor, his face drooping as he thought.

"Don't start talking about how nice the office is, or any of those distracting tactics you sometimes try. I don't have the patience to suffer through them today. Just tell me, why are you here?"

William braced himself. "I need you to take all of them with you back to Kar'm."

"No," replied Christina. "I was going to bring them back to you, but you're here now. I have my own world of problems. Something's wrong in Kar'm, and I have to get a handle on it."

"Mineau's not safe," said William, looking up at her, his eyes sharing some of the horror he'd seen.

Christina shook her head. "Did you hear about the airship bombing at the palaces of Myke? Nowhere is safe these days, Will. Tee, Elly, even Mounira, they've proven themselves to be quite capable. Take them with you, it sounds like you need all the help you can get."

"I can't," said William, insistently. "I can't take them."

Christina stood up in frustration. "That's not an

answer. You can't just keep refusing information and relying on my sense of morality to backstop all of this. Not this time."

William put his head in his hands. "You must have seen the Red Hoods around, right? They aren't with Pieman. They're with Caterina Maurice."

"We ran into one at Elly's house. He wore an old-style Fare cloak. What does this have to do with anything?" asked Christina.

"I think..." he paused and scratched his beard. "I think she's got all the royals, even the one's the Piemans got over-thrown, behind them. They were shipping people off from Minette and Mineau to Kaban."

"Slavers?"

William nodded, his eyes filled with unspoken guilt.

Christina's eyes moved around the room as she put the pieces together. "Jennifer, and Elly's parents?"

He nodded again.

She sat quietly, trying not to think of all the horrible stories she'd heard about Kaban and how they treated slaves, particularly northern ones. "Where's the Tub in all of this?"

William shook his head. "Almost all of my usual contacts are dead, missing or working for the other side. I haven't heard from my dad in months. I'm on my own."

"The kids can help," offered Christina half-heartedly.

He looked at her, tears in his eyes. She lowered her

gaze in agreement.

"I was hoping to find Bakon and Egelina-Marie here, to have them come with me, but I was told you guys haven't seen them."

Christina shook her head. "Sorry."

William threw up his hands. "Well, that's it then. That's why. I have to go after Jennifer and the others. I can't abandon them."

"No, you can't go after them," countered Christina. "You know history as well as I do, you can't go to Kaban. They are lost and gone. You have a moral obligation to *not* make Tee an orphan."

"And what about Elly? What about the lives of all of those people, who were my friends and neighbors? How can I just go on knowing that I did nothing?" he asked, tears streaming down. "*How?*"

Christina stared at the floor between them. "I'll do the best I can with the kids. It's only going to make things in Kar'm more complicated."

"I understand," he said wiping his nose on a handkerchief. "And thank you." He stood and walked over to the door. "I'd better get going."

She turned, her head shaking. "You can't do this alone."

"Maybe I'll find some along the road," he replied with a half-smile.

"What road is that?" she asked.

"The road to redemption."

CHAPTER EIGHT
WATT SHINES BRIGHTLY

Ruffo stared nervously at Franklin. "You really think this is going to work? I mean, that's a freaking guarded manor over there. It's practically a castle. Are you even allowed to just walk up to those?"

Gesturing to Stefano and Ruffo's new clothes, Franklin said, "I was right about the card games, wasn't I? I know what I'm doing. Do you like how you look now? You gentlemen need to simply consider this like knocking on the door of an establishment... sorry, place... that has someone in it who owes you money. Be firm, but not rude. Show *some* class."

Stefano nodded as he wrapped his mind around it. "I get it. Hey, thanks, that actually helped, Franky. Huh." He smiled at his long time buddy.

Ruffo gave Franklin a light punch in the arm, having learned the amount the kid could take the day before. "Three days, and now you're starting to make some sense when you talk."

The thugs sauntered up to the iron bars of the portcullis, with Franklin walking a few feet behind them. Ruffo picked up a stick and, even though one of the guards was staring squarely at him, proceeded to bang it along the bars. "Hey, excuse me, anyone home?" he asked loudly.

Franklin rolled his eyes. "Here's goes everything," he muttered.

"State your business," commanded the guard. He was wearing light chainmail armor and a helmet with a wide metal brim. Franklin was surprised to see the guard wearing the colors of Staaten, for they were technically in Elizabetina. He wondered if something had happened, and found himself missing home for a moment. He 'd always kept up to date on the latest events there.

"I've got...ah... I've got Franklin..." Ruffo froze, sweating. He glanced back at Franklin with panic in his eyes.

Stefano hit him in the shoulder and picked up the slack. "We've got Franklin Charles David Watt here to see your guy, Simon St. Malo," he said. He smiled proudly that he'd made it through the giant mouthful successfully.

Two more guards approached the portcullis. After a quick discussion, one bellowed, "Go away!"

Ruffo and Stefano glanced back at Franklin.

"Imagine someone in there with something you

want," he reminded them. He crossed his fingers.

Stefano nodded and walked right up to the iron bars. "Um, listen. You've got what, a half-dozen archers and some riflemen around? Do we look like a threat? We're just two guys and a kid. But this kid? He's a genius that *your* genius guy's been looking for. I'm not saying he's an Abominator or nothing, I'm just saying that your guy wanted to talk to him. So, here he is. For talking."

The guards chatted amongst themselves.

Ruffo glanced about, as if he was concerned that someone might overhear him. "Hey guys, come here." He motioned for the guards to join him right up close. "Look, we don't want this to get messy. Here's a little something." He dropped a few small coin pouches as Franklin had expected. "You know, to cover any lost wages in having to help us, right? This is no bribe or nothing, it's just covering what we figure you fine gentlemen are paid. Just a friendly thank you, really."

Franklin couldn't believe his ears as they filled with the sound of the portcullis going up.

———————

Alfrida carefully opened the door to Simon's study. It had been a rocky several weeks since the Regent Caterina had appointed her to replace Cleeves. Simon's fear of the Lady in Red had visibly restrained his temper long enough for him to realize that Alfrida was truly excellent at what she did. As much as he believed her to be spying on him for Caterina, he appreciated things like pots of tea appearing out of nowhere when he wanted them.

She listened intently before stepping in. She rarely entered in the early afternoon, and didn't want to surprise him. "High Conventioneer St. Malo?" she called out softly, creeping in. She slowly made her way through the labyrinth of bookcases until she found Simon at one of his workbenches, asleep. He was surrounded by an astounding mass of crumbled up papers and a strange vertical black board with white writing on it. The top of his greasy head of salt and pepper hair was all that was visible at first.

Sounding like a dragon awakening at the start of a bad mood, Simon grumbled. "Are you wondering about the board?" he asked, rubbing his face. "That was the gift from Conventioneer Pillans. It's what you had those animals haul in last week... I'm surprised those men didn't knock over *every* bookcase in here. I decided to assemble it last night. Please send a thank you basket or whatever to James for me." He scratched his head and chin vigorously and then stopped, and gazed at the blackboard. "It's a good little invention. The man sees the simple things that are needed. The chalk is easy to make, too, at least according to his notes." Simon tossed papers into the air until he found what he wanted. "Here, make lots. Even..." he bit his tongue to keep from insulting her. "Never mind."

Alfrida nodded and took the paper from him. With a repulsive sniff, she asked, "Have you... bathed yet sir?

It's been—"

Simon frowned. "I don't have *time* for anything, save for eating, and barely that. But you know that, don't you, *spy?* Are you testing me?"

With a sigh, she repeated once again, "I am not a spy. I am here to help you, sir." She straightened her long coat and bow tie, and then fixed her pony-tail. "Appearance is important. Particularly when one has an unexpected visitor."

"What type of idiot shows up at this hour of the morning?" asked Simon, rubbing his face. "I have no time for them. Shoot them or send them away, I don't care."

Alfrida raised a finger, drawing his attention. "Firstly, it is early afternoon, sir. And secondly, he is accompanied by two men of significant size, and is apparently a genius of some note."

Simon growled. "Unless these men are giants and the other one is dragging his massive brain behind him, I don't care."

"His name is Franklin something Watt, I'm told," she said.

He started shooing her away. "Shoot them, throw them out, whatever. Fetch me some tea and a new shirt if you can, you seem to be behind on knowing what I want."

Deciding to push even further, Alfrida asked gently, "Isn't Watt the name of one of the inventors you have retained?"

He looked at her blankly. "Hold on." He took a moment to get his mental bearings. "Did you say Franklin Watt? Is he a teenage boy?"

"Yes, sir. I've seen him myself. Likely fifteen or sixteen years old, and about your height. Dark blond hair, black eye, well dressed."

Simon glared at the twenty-year-old woman, tapping his fingers on the workbench. "Bring him in."

"Immediately, sir?" she asked, looking at his wrinkled and tea stained shirt.

"I have no time for anything else."

"I could arrange things so that you have time for the bath that is already poured."

"So you *are* ahead of me. Fine. I'll be there in a moment." Simon glanced at the number of days remaining he'd scrawled in the upper corner of his workbench. It was bad enough that he hadn't made any significant headway deciphering Klaus' plans the Lady had left him.

There was a loud knock at the study's door. Simon finished neatening his workbench and started making his way to the front seating area. "Come!" he bellowed.

Alfrida opened the door and stepped in. "I present Franklin Charles David Watt, son of the inventor Maxwell Watt." She ushered Franklin in and closed the door behind them.

Simon studied the boy as he took in the grandeur of the study. It was almost the size of the royal library, which was only a few miles away. Its thirty-foot ceiling and skylights made it seem unbelievably large, with bookcases along the wall from floor to ceiling and eight-foot bookcases everywhere in-between.

"Tea?" asked Alfrida.

"I don't expect Master Watt to be staying that long," said Simon sharply.

"I do," retorted Franklin with the same sharpness. Simon was shorter than he'd expected, but his eyes seem to be reading everything.

"Careful boy. The grey suits you, I hear it's quite the rage at the moment. Though I have to say, it looks a bit big on you, and given the weather, it must be a tad hot, is it not? If you were trying to impress me, you've failed, but it clearly impressed the guards."

Franklin tried hiding his shaking hands behind his back.

"Now, the more intriguing question for me," continued Simon, "is how did you end up with enough money for all of that?" he said, gesturing to the boy's outfit. "I know your father well enough, and I know Klaus doesn't have such wealth, so where could you have acquired money?"

"I... I have my ways. Which was why LeLoup was

bringing me to meet you," said Franklin, trying to keep his voice firm and confident.

Simon started walking in a slow circle around Franklin. "Oh, really? Now, why would Andre LeLoup do that? Given that he's dead, it makes your story a bit less plausible."

Franklin pointed at the door. "He's not dead. Just ask Ruffo and Stefano, they were his henchmen. He'd be here, but... he abandoned us to hunt Tee again."

"Who's Tee?" asked Simon.

"Tee Baker," replied Franklin.

Simon shrugged. "Doesn't ring a bell."

"She's the granddaughter of Nikolas Klaus," said Franklin nervously.

"Oh, Nikolas Klaus? What do you know of that long-dead inventor?" asked Simon, his words like poisoned velvet. There weren't many who knew that Nikolas hadn't died long ago. Marcus had covered up his death so that he could live a seemingly free life, something Simon hadn't ever understood but figured there was a sinister reason behind it somewhere. Marcus wasn't the altruistic type.

Franklin squirmed and rubbed his hands together. "I met Klaus. He's bald and has a salt and pepper beard. You have him on a painting in the corridor, along with a young you and someone else. I was briefly in Klaus' lab before it burned down."

Simon laughed. "Are we making up more stories, then? Well, I have a magic pony that breathes fire and is running for parliament in Freland," he replied, his sarcasm absolutely biting.

Franklin felt a lump grow in his throat. Simon had a way of seeping into one's bones. His movements and tone, his words and expressions, made Franklin feel like he was prey being stalked. "No, it's true! Look, I know where the steam engine plans are. Do you want them or not?" he asked, gesturing wildly.

Simon stopped circling and studied the boy. He rubbed his forehead, wondering about everything that had been said. "Why would I want the steam engine plans when I have your father?"

Franklin glanced around nervously. "Because… because I know my father, he wouldn't help you," he stammered. "You need the plans, that's why you came after them in the first place."

"I did? I don't remember visiting Inglea. Are you sure it wasn't someone else?" Simon moved his head from side to side, wondering a bit more how to allow this scene to play itself out. "Klaus, LeLoup, the steam engine plans. You have an ever-growing list of make-believe."

Taking a slow breath, Franklin gave Simon a steely glare that caught the man off guard. "When I was in Klaus' lab, I saw a mechanical arm prototype. I saw a rocket cart of his fly through the sky, and I've ridden on a

King's-Horse with Christina Creangle. What more proof do you want?"

"Wait," said Simon, putting his hand up. The ring of truth was too loud for him to ignore. "Let's go back to the steam engine plans. What do you want for them, your father's release?"

Franklin stared at the ground, confused by why the very thought hadn't occurred to him. "I... I figured you wouldn't do that," he replied.

"And I'm going to guess you're really after something more interesting, aren't you? I'd be willing to allow a visit. But what is it you truly want?"

"I want money," said Franklin, looking up. "I have two guys who have kept me alive that I promised money to."

Simon gestured to Franklin's clothes. "It seems that you already have a way to make money. Why do you need some from me? I can give you some for the plans, but that's not really it. What do you _want_?"

A smile crept out of Franklin. "I want to change the world."

"Ah, there it is," said Simon, pointing. "And as for those two men, I'll have them killed. I have no need for them."

"No," said Franklin startled.

Simon laughed. "You're in no position to negotiate."

"They're with me," he said, surprised at himself.

"They're my friends. You have lots of men, if they cause trouble you can have them killed."

Simon folded his arms. "How badly do you want to change the world?"

"More than anything."

Taking a moment to reconsider what he was about to say, Simon figured it was worth the risk. "How about a little test? If you've really been to Klaus' lab, then you should have no problem deciphering some plans I have of his. You have one day to tell me how it works."

"And if I can't?" asked Franklin, shifting from foot to foot nervously.

"Then I'll get the plans out of you, then have you buried," said Simon with a twisted smile. "And I'll allow your friends to live, either way."

Franklin swallowed hard. "Okay, deal."

CHAPTER NINE
DRAGON AND FOX

Years ago, a two and a half year-old Richy ran as fast as he could, in and out of the bushes and small trees of their yard, his older sister hot on his trail.

"I'm going to get you!" yelled eight-year-old Amami happily. She had a leafy stick of bamboo between her legs, a floppy black cloth tied around her neck, and a toy sword in her rope belt. "You'll never get away, Dragon! I will catch you!"

Richy squealed. "No, Fox! No, you not!"

As he tore past his father, the grey haired man smiled. He'd been gardening for hours, and couldn't get enough of it. His memories of life in Inglea had faded to the point of feeling like stories that had been told to him, rather than ones he'd lived. Out of the corner of his eye, he caught sight of Amami and tucked his head down. Amami let go of the bamboo stick, planted her hands on his back, flipped over him, landed, and continued, never having broken her rhythm. He bent down to pick up his hat and her stick. "Where do you get that from, Amy?" he wondered.

His wife, Tsuruko, shook her head. She didn't approve of letting Amami do such things. She found them disrespectful, but she knew there was no coming between a father and daughter.

"Careful Amy!" he yelled, earning a nod from his wife.

"You too, Riichi. Right, Everett?" added Tsuruko.

"Yes, you too, Richy," he replied with a smile. He'd never managed to get the hang of pronouncing Richy's name properly, but Tsuruko didn't seem to mind his Ingleash version.

"Sorry, Daddy! But I'm chasing a sneaky dragon! Come here! The Fox is going to get you!" Amami yelled in a mix of languages. As Richy slid under a bench, Amami sprang over it, landing with her sword in hand and catching her brother by surprise.

Tsuruko smiled. She didn't show it often, but she was proud of her daughter. She was fearless. "She must get that from you, Ev," she said.

After Everett Waxman had been disowned by his family, he'd headed as far east as he could. At the feet of the great Eastern Mountains, he'd learned the languages of the dispersed communities and made a living trading goods from village to village. It was a simple life, devoid of the politics and noise that had surrounded him in Inglea.

Standing on a rocky hill one late afternoon, staring at the towering Eastern Mountains, he'd watched a dot in the distance approach and become something indescribable. As it shot past him leaving a black smoke trail in the sky, he knew he had to follow it. Abandoning his cart, he took off on his horse. There, in a crashed contraption unlike anything he'd ever seen, he found a woman at death's door. After nursing Tsuruko back to health, they'd built a home on the very spot.

"Ev?" asked Tsuruko, shaking her head. She knew that look in his eyes. It was one of the many things she loved about him, how the past stayed so alive inside him.

"Hmm? Sorry, my dear. Did you say something?" he replied.

She smiled at him in response.

He gazed up at the sun to get a sense of the time. "How about I go in and make lunch?" He planted his trowel and dusted off his hands. "I'll check on the water pumps later."

Tsuruko stretched her back and watched the kids dodge expertly around the vegetables, rain barrels and wheelbarrows. She took a moment to fix her long black hair back into a proper pony-tail. "I'll check them now. I am concerned about the underground river water level. The spring has been too dry."

"You're always worried about something, Tsu," said her husband.

"There is always something about which we can despair," she replied.

"Argh! Your homeland has such depressing philosophers to quote. It's bad enough to read them, but hearing them is worse," he said, half-joking.

"If you think that, then you still don't understand them," she said, a mock look of disapproval on her face. "How did I go from reaching for the sky, to being happy on the ground with you?"

"Because, I come from a long line of windbags. So I give you the sky and the ground, together," he said, giving her a kiss. "Careful Amy!" He shook his head. "Our children will be the end of me, I swear it."

Tsuruko laughed and tapped his chest. "Lunch?"

"Lunch," he replied.

As Tsuruko opened the cellar doors and walked inside, she smiled at the old water pumps. What they didn't salvage from her flying ship to make the pumps, they'd used in the house or as decorations in the yard. She checked the gauges and dials.

Everett jumped as Tsuruko tapped his arm, his deep blue eyes focusing. "You scared me. Weren't you checking the pumps?"

"I did. I called to you as I approached, but you didn't hear me," she said, concerned. Maybe his increasing tendency to daydream was more than just loving life. "Did the mountains steal your soul again?"

He chuckled. "No. But you know, they aren't alive. They can't do that"

"That's not what my ancestors say," she said hugging him.

"Really? I didn't know that."

"No, I am joking," she replied. "How is my... sarcasm?"

"It's getting there," he said giving her a kiss.

"I worry about you sometimes."

"I'm just... I don't know. I haven't heard from my brother in a while. I hope he finds happiness one day, figures out how to get away from the affairs of the Tub and Fare and the royals, and just have a life he can appreciate. You know? Just be who he is, enjoy the dirt, enjoy being alive."

"You worry about things you cannot change."

Suddenly, both kids screamed. Tsuruko and Everett bolted to the other side of their one story home.

At the edge of their land, where the grass turned back to dusty, hard soil, stood a man in his sixties. He had a full head of grey hair, a white shirt with frilly sleeves and beige pants. Despite the heat, over top he had a beige jacket that went halfway down to his calves. His presence and intensity gave them pause. Behind him were three men with camels, all dressed for desert riding, and clearly local.

Tsuruko put her trembling arms around her

whimpering children and pulled them back to the front door. They'd fended off raiders before, but this felt entirely different. "We have nothing. Go away."

"My name is Marcus Pieman," said the man in a passable local accent.

"Pieman?" whispered Everett, worried. He'd heard the name before from his father before, long ago.

Marcus continued, "I didn't mean to scare the children. I have come seeking the truth to a local legend. It is said that once, years ago, there was a streak in the sky. It was said to be a metal bird from over the Eastern Mountains, and that it died in a ball of flame. But no signs of it seem to exist, and everyone points in different directions as to where it might have crashed. My search has led me here."

Everett glanced at the camel-riders, all were armed with pistols. "Never heard of it," he said sternly. "Please leave. This is our property."

Taking a step forward, Marcus said, "This flying thing, I've heard it called the Hotaru. I'm told that means firefly. While others might think your little green oasis here in the desert is luck or from hard work, I am more than just an inventor, I am a leader of our kind. I know innovation when I see it, and there is no doubt in my mind that all of this," he gestured at the thriving oasis, "is tied to the Hotaru. I have been to Olsmos in the north, and to the border of Endera in the south. There is nothing like this home of yours. So, please, do not insult me. I need to know what you know, and to have what remains of it."

"Leave," insisted Everett, pulling out a flintlock rifle hidden in the front door frame. He aimed it at Marcus.

Marcus rubbed between his eyes, thinking. "Everett, right? Everett Waxman. Son of Alan Waxman, former leader of the Tub. I met your father on a couple of occasions. Interesting man. Flat head, bulbous nose, gregarious."

Everett shrugged. "So, you've met him, am I to be impressed? All the more reason for you to leave us alone. Do you see a flying ship around here? No, so go." He shook the rifle. "Leave!" Concern spread across his face as he saw the camel-men standing there, pistols still in hand but not pointed at him. How dangerous *was* this man?

Marcus glanced down at the grassy border at his feet. "There are several ways in which I could get what I'm looking for. Few of them have happy endings. Tsuruko, is it? I hope I am pronouncing your name correctly."

She stared at him, and after a moment of hesitation, gave him a confirming nod.

"Good," he replied. "I see the worry in your motherly eyes. Hotaru means something to you. Please, spare everyone grief and tell me what you know. I'm starting to lose my patience."

Tsuruko shot a glance to her husband as the wheels

turned in her mind. "It does not exist anymore. There is no Hotaru. It's pieces. It became part of all this," she said, pointing at the garden. "I have nothing to share with you. It is gone, long ago."

Marcus scratched the back of his neck and put his spectacles on. "That's disappointing. You will show me every piece, then."

"We will do no such thing," said Everett, fuming. "We want nothing to do with your Tubs and Fares and *nonsense*."

Staring at Everett to the point of making him take a half step back, Marcus stepped on to the grass. "'A man can no more run from his destiny as he can dig his way out of a hole.' Luther Siler, Ingleash philosopher. You studied him, didn't you?" He put his hands in the pockets of his pant. On the surface, Marcus seemed harmless, save for the intensity that emanated from him. Bowing his head, he sighed. "What I'm doing, I'm doing for the good of our kind. Every genius, inventor, scientist, everyone called an Abominator because they dare to pursue knowledge, to knock on the door of the impossible. You might have run away from the world, Everett, but I... I am changing it, and the Hotaru is key."

"Leave," insisted Everett, raising his rifle.

Marcus pulled out his pocket-watch and stared at it pensively. "I don't have time for this. Enough with trying to be pleasant. Understand that this will be the last time you'll see me. You'll be dealing with representatives of mine from here on out."

Tsuruko stepped forward. "It was destroyed, long ago. I crashed out of the sky."

"Did you invent it?" he asked.

She stared at Everett, who was shaking his head. "Yes."

"And you piloted it over the Eastern Mountains on your own?" he pressed.

"No. I went through most of it. The Hotaru, it graces the wind, it moves well."

"Tsu, you shouldn't—" said Everett, but she waved him off.

"Impressive." Marcus stared at the ground in thought. "You will build me one."

Everett fired at Marcus' chest, knocking him clean off his feet. The bullet bounced off the armor below his shirt and scratched his eye.

Before Marcus could signal them to stop, one of the camel-men shot Everett in the shoulder, dropping him to the ground. Standing back up, his hand over his bleeding eye, Marcus glared at Tsuruko. "That will cost you dearly. There will be no opportunity for rebellion," he said. He turned to the camel-men. "Take the boy."

"No!" screamed Tsuruko. Two of the camel-men took aim at Amami and Everett, while the third scooped up Richy.

"You'll get your son back *after* you've built me a working Hotaru," said Marcus, taking a cloth from a saddle bag and putting it over his eye.

Tsuruko dropped to her knees, her hands clasped. "No! Please no! I cannot! I cannot build you a working one!"

"Do I need to kill your son, here, in front of you, to motivate you properly?" asked Marcus, his white shirt and beige pants wet with blood.

"I cannot make the engine! I never built it and it was destroyed in the crash. I know how to make everything else, but not that. I can make the body, but not the heart."

Marcus waved away the camel-men. "Fine. Everything else you need, you will have. You have one year, after which, I make no promises about your boy."

"Riichi!" screamed Amami as he was bound and gagged.

———————⌐———————

Richy stared at the jail cell wall. Since the Lady in Red had ordered him taken away Eg and Bakon, he'd lost track of time. He'd clawed scratches into the cell's soft stone wall to help keep track of time. He'd been there a few weeks already.

The other three cells in the jail were empty, each equipped with the same straw mattress, stone walls and small windows at the back for air and light. Richy wondered if someone had made one jail design and copied it everywhere, because it looked exactly like the one in Minette.

Falling asleep had been hard in the hot and humid cell, but every time he started to drift off the rowdy guards down the hall woke up him with their yelling.

He started at the three crank lanterns hanging in the middle of the room. Below them was a desk which was only used by the guards to put their mugs of ale on before they started tormenting him, a daily source of amusement for them.

Sometimes they'd throw water at him, sometimes they'd just call him names, and a few times they'd poked him with his own shock-sticks. He'd almost grabbed one once, and would have been more than happy to show them it was a lot more than a simple metal stick.

The door to the office never closed properly, and the day's summer breeze was bringing their voices in clearly.

"In the morning, I've got a meeting with the new magistrate. I hear he might be open to selling the exotic kid to the Kaban ambassador," said a deep, aggressive voice Richy knew all too well. His name was Bernardo, and he was a short, heavily-bearded man with a huge, twisted personality.

Though Bernardo was the youngest of the half-dozen guards of the town, he'd become the ring-leader in recent weeks, taking advantage of the chaos and darker side of human nature. Richy'd heard there was a red-hooded advisor accompanying the new magistrate everywhere he went. He wondered if the Red Hood was connected to the Lady in Red. If so, she was much more powerful than he'd imagined.

Gunter scratched his old, tired face. He'd worked with Bernardo for years, and men just like him for decades. They played with fire until they got burned. "Bernardo, though you know well about such things, I think…"

"Yes?" asked Bernardo, the giant awaiting the advice of the mouse.

"Don't you think that selling people is wrong? I mean, it's slavery. We stopped that here in Laros a long, long time ago." Gunter's voice was laced with hopelessness, but the fragment of his noble soul that remained had to speak up. He'd always been the one to bring Richy a towel when they'd doused him with water, or give him the tray of food if Bernardo had left it just out of reach.

"I'm surprised at you, Gunter," said Bernardo condescendingly. "Do you really think that's what the Kaban do? It isn't slavery at all. They just allow people an opportunity to have purpose and fulfillment, while they earn their way to citizenship in that paradise."

"But they have no freedom, no—"

Bernardo gave Gunter a shove. "Do any of us really have freedom? You have a home with a leaking roof and mold on the walls, I've seen it. Where is your freedom to get rid of that? Others are getting rich every day out there. What if you could trade this boy for some of that? For a house that didn't leak, for food on the table every night? He's young, he'll survive. If he doesn't, who's to say that he wouldn't have died on his own?"

"I think—"

Grabbing Gunter by the collar, Bernardo growled at him. "I'm trying to make you feel better, old man. Careful you don't end up on the cart to Kaban *with* the kid. Got it?"

"Yes... yes, I understand," said Gunter, cowering.

A gunshot, and then another, cracked the night. Richy sprang to his feet and crossed the cell. He grabbed the bars and strained to listen. Several more shots rang out down the corridor. He could hear Bernardo cursing and struggling with someone. "Don't hurt the old man!" yelled Richy. "Is that you, Bakon? Eg? I'm over here! Don't hurt the old man, though!" His heart was racing.

He grabbed his yellow cloak and put it on, hoping that any stray bullets would find it instead of him. Suddenly, a lantern shattered, and then another.

"Eg? Bakon?" called out Richy, his voice trembling. His almond-shaped blue eyes squinted in the dim light as he backed up. Instinctively, he reached into the pockets of his cloak, only to be reminded his shock-sticks weren't there. Something was moving in the shadows. The moonlight bounced off of two long blades. "Who are you?

What do you want?"

A female voice asked something forcefully.

"I don't understand. Do you speak Frelish?" asked Richy, his hands in tight fists.

"Dragon?"

"What? Who are you? Why are you here?" asked Richy.

The silhouette unlocked his cell door and gently pushed it open. She was about the same size as him, her head and body hidden behind a dark hood and cloak. She raised empty hands.

"Your hood, pull it back," said the woman in angry Frelish. "I mean you no harm, but I must see your face. I need to know if you are the blue-eyed dragon."

"What? I'm just a kid," he said, glancing around.

"Show me your face... please."

With a deep breath, he complied and looked at her blankly.

"Riichi!" she said, leaping forward and hugging him.

Without a thought, a name long forgotten rocketed out of him, "Amami?"

CHAPTER TEN

Lost Beauties

"Belly! Belly! Banging! Banging at the door!" yelled a terrified little Selvin. He shook his sleeping older brother as vigorously as he could. "Wake up!"

Beldon sat up, squinting. "You were just having a nightmare, Skelly. It's dark. Go back to bed."

"Scary," said the second outline beside his bed.

"It's okay, Bore," said Beldon, patting his little brother on the head. Then he stiffened as he heard screams coming from downstairs. "What's that?"

"Don't know," said little Selvin.

"Okay," said Beldon, slipping out of his bed and tiptoeing to their bedroom door. Opening it a crack, he peeked out. He saw smoke and people running about.

He stared at his brothers, trying to hide his panic. Selvin was still looking sickly, having nearly drowned a second time two weeks ago.

"Mama?" asked Bore.

"That's what I'm thinking, Bore," said Beldon. "Maybe she needs our help."

"We go help?" asked Selvin.

Beldon nodded.

Holding their hands in a chain, they opened the door.

An hour later, Caterina stumbled up to the boys' room, the ruined manor still alive with the sounds of fighting and a raging fire. She dropped her mother's short sword, covered in the blood of her husband, and stared at the broken lock on the bedroom door. She stepped into the room, her eyes darting about. "Boys?!" she screamed, as she ran from bed to bed. She squinted in the meager light, hunting around for a lantern to crank. With lantern in hand, she checked under each bed and behind the curtains. "Bel? Sel? Bore? Come out, Mama's not playing."

Wiping her tears, she picked up the blade and ran down the corridor, checking every bedroom and screaming for her boys until the smoke became too thick to speak. As she retreated to the back of the manor, she searched every nook and cranny along the way, her voice becoming hoarse in the process. Stepping over bodies and fending off angry peasants at each turn, she found herself regretting much of her life.

She'd followed her father's plan, ever the dutiful daughter, even though she thought it insane. She'd never dreamed it could cost her the life of her sons. She'd never questioned her beliefs and life until now. His plan to have her home stormed by an angry mob was intended to drive a permanent wedge of fear between the Ahemian royals and the Piemans.

———————

The next morning, Gaston found her standing among the ashes of their once beautiful home. She was dressed in the tatters from the night before, filthy from head to foot. She twitched at the sound of his malevolent voice as he went on about necessary sacrifices and how the leaders of the One True Fare, as he called it, were pleased with her. He droned on about the destiny one is given versus the life we hope to have. As he reached to put his arm on her shoulder, she stabbed him through the heart with her mother's short sword. She quickly pulled the sword out and stabbed him several more times, screaming.

She glared up at the Fare representatives, all standing about with looks of shock and horror. They turned to one another, some gesturing to their coaches while others pointing at her.

Finally, one short and sheepish man stepped forward. He tried to remove his spectacles, only to drop them to the ground. Nervously he groped about for them. He stood slowly, as if any sudden action might cause Caterina to strike.

"Duchess Catherine, you look cold," he said, trying his best not to stare at Gaston's body or her bloody sword.

She stared at him blankly.

The man turned and gestured to a servant, who

quickly brought him a folded new, red cloak. He walked over to hand it to her and froze as he realized he'd stepped in a puddle of Gaston's blood.

Caterina reached out and took the cloak from him. Her eyes followed the man has he hurried back to his pack. She then turned her attention to the embroidery on the cloak. It denoted the wearer as a Fare leader, one who reported directly to the Fare's inner council. She looked up at her audience with a new respect and understanding.

Stepping over her father's body, she donned the cloak. "Duchess Catherine is dead. Destiny has made me simply a lady in red."

Caterina hadn't spoken to Bakon or Egelina-Marie for the entire trip from Wosa to the Staaten capital city of Andrea. Her mind was on a mix of her duties as Regent of Staaten, and trying to make sense of finding Beldon alive. Rather than happiness, she felt irritation at the distraction he represented. Secretly, both she and Bakon wished she'd never stroked his earlobe and removed all possibility of doubt.

She stood before the door of the two floor apartment she'd had Bakon and Egelina-Marie put in. Part of her wanted to leave, to have them simply killed and pretend as if none of it had happened, yet she couldn't, at least not yet. With hesitation, she knocked.

Bakon opened the door, expecting to see yet another

guard offering them food or reminding them that they were free to tour the grounds—accompanied. They hadn't ventured out since arriving, instead preferring to talk and sit on the balcony.

"Hello, Bel—Bakon," said Caterina, pulling her hood back. She had the same pained expression on her face as he did. "Care to join me for a walk?"

Bakon nodded, unable to find words. He glanced back at Eg who gestured her support. They both knew he had no choice; one does not deny the Regent anything in their homeland.

They walked in awkward silence through the brilliantly colorful western garden. Bakon dared a glance at her out of the corner of his eye. The grey streak in her thin, dark hair and the scar from her eye to her chin added to the sense that she was someone built over the remains of his mother. She had an unnerving air in place of the warmth he remembered.

She caught his gaze and held it. Her question was obvious.

"The nanny came in that night and snuck us out. We traveled west for a while. We had little money or money... It was terrifying," said Bakon, grimacing. He hated thinking about those times. It made him feel weak and small inside.

"For a while? So the nanny abandoned the three of you?" asked Caterina. Her words were slow and her face pained, as if she were walking barefoot on broken glass.

Bakon's face twisted as he tried to jerk loose the answers from his memory. He stared at the river-rock pathway as they entered the shadow of a small forest, still within the confines of the garden. "I didn't know until recently that she'd planned to sell us to the Ginger Lady. She didn't though, for some reason."

"How do you know that?"

"There was a note in the Ginger Lady's house. That's where I saw the name Beldon... Beldon Pieman," he replied, his throat tight with emotion. He took out the note and handed it to her.

Caterina's hands shook as she read. "I'll hunt her down," she said through clenched teeth. "That—"

Bakon cut her off. "If you're saying that for me, don't. She didn't put us in the hands of the Ginger Lady. We ended up with Nikolas and Isabella Klaus... by Fate, I guess. They were wonderful, and we were quite a handful."

Caterina stopped and gazed into the forest. "What's your relationship with Abeland Pieman? You were traveling with him."

Rolling his shoulders, Bakon couldn't help feeling like their walk was becoming an interrogation. "I met him on the road. He wasn't making any sense, and looked really rough when I found him. He took me to his old house and I got cleaned up. Then shortly after, we ran into you."

He could feel her glaring at him, radiating fear and intimidation.

"You aren't working with him?" she asked.

Bakon looked around. "No, but even if I was, he ditched me. So, why would I be loyal to him? "

She nodded and moved on. "Are your brothers alive?"

"They were in Mineau before the attack. I think so... I hope so," he said.

"Mineau?" She turned away, rubbing her face at the realization. "Have you heard from them?"

Bakon shook his head. "I haven't heard anything about what's happened back home."

"Your girlfriend called you Bakon, why is that? You know your name is Beldon now, so why don't you correct her?"

"Can I speak frankly, your highness?" he asked, annoyed. He stared at her, wondering why the gulf between them felt like it was just getting wider.

Caterina gestured to the empty shadows. "Go ahead."

"I *am* Bakon Cochon, I *was* Beldon Pieman... Maurice, whatever."

She stared at him, thinking. "Why the name Bakon?"

"That's what our nanny called me all the time. I'm Bakon, and my brothers are Squeals and Bore. I didn't remember their real names until I saw the note."

She handed the note back and looked at him. With a wave to the shadows, she said, "That will be all, thank you. I need only one of you to take him back to his room." She turned to Bakon. "Thank you."

CHAPTER ELEVEN
YOU CAN NEVER
GO HOME

Tee sprang out of the cart, happy for their crazy ride to be over. It had taken a couple of days and some ingenuity to rig a cart to the back of the King's-Horse. Several times they'd had to stop along the way to make repairs, but it had pretty much worked.

The noise in the cart had been so thunderous as to make talking with Elly impossible. Instead, Tee had spent much of the journey thinking about her Grandpapa's armband grapple device he'd made for Franklin, which she'd seen Franklin sketching in Minette. Wanting to reclaim that from Franklin in a way, she decided she'd make her own, and, in doing so, bring her Grandpapa a bit closer to her. The sight of the ruined castle of Kar'm coming into view got her hopeful she'd be able to find a small corner somewhere and build it.

Waiting for them was a towering, muscular man wearing only a leather vest, shorts and sandals. He was bald, with a pointy, orange beard that looked like fury escaping through his chin. He had a battle-axe on his back and a huge pistol on his thick belt. He broke into a pained smile at the sight of Christina running up to give him a hug.

"Husband?" asked Tee to Mounira.

"Not exactly," she replied. "I think they're *sort of* married, but—"

"Later," whispered Tee as Christina waved them over.

Tee and Mounira went to the cart to help get Elly out.

"Let me help," said the muscly man. "I'm Remy Silskin." He picked Elly up and put her down gently. "You alright?"

"I'm fine," replied Elly.

"He's huge," said Tee, staring at him.

"He can hear you," said Remi.

"It's probably okay. If he's talking in the third person, he can't be that bright," joked Tee.

Everyone went quiet.

Angelina whistled as she came out of hiding. "Wow, she's got your number, Remi."

Christina laughed. "She's Sam Baker's granddaughter, Remi. Recognize anything?"

He grumbled as he gazed down at the petite girl with the huge brown eyes. "Wow, the eyes and the razor tongue. We better put a sign on her: Warning!—Baker—

may cause burns."

Everyone laughed.

"Angelina, can you carefully take Elly in? Have Francis check her wounds. I'm sure everything's fine, but I'd like to know for sure."

"Did you say Franklin?" asked Tee, worried.

"What?" said Christina, momentarily confused. "No, Francis, Doctor Francis Stein. He's my lead medical scientist. Whenever someone shows up seriously wounded, I have him check them out. Nothing special."

"We should ask him about the painkillers we made," said Mounira to Elly, who nodded in agreement. "Do you think he has a different way to do it? I'm thinking—"

"Mounira?" asked Elly.

"Yes?" replied Mounira.

"Quiet time," said Elly, in her best impression of an older sister.

Mounira glanced around. "Okay,"

After everyone had left, Christina turned to Remi. "I know that look in your eyes, and Angelina's. What's going on?"

Remy frowned, his shoulders rolled forward. "We had a small problem, but it's been dealt with."

"What type of problem? There are a lot of *small* problems lately," she said.

He tugged lightly on his goatee. "We found a satchel

of notes about what we were doing and who was here. We don't know who made them, but we found who took it. At least, Angelina thinks we did. Also, one of Canny's men went missing for a day and didn't offer an explanation of where he'd been. Canny guessed he went for a walk to relieve some stress. Things haven't been going at all well here over the past two weeks."

"How does Angelina tie into this?" asked Christina.

His face stiffened. "She found the satchel, brought it to me, we argued. We're doing that a lot, lately. She decided to go out riding with a few others and found a dead guy she recognized. He had some papers stuffed in his pockets, the content similar to what was in the satchel. She found him about two miles east of here, neck broken."

Christina stared at the ground. "Angelina went out riding? She hates that."

Remy shrugged.

"That doesn't make sense. If the guy's neck was broken—" said Christina.

"He was at the bottom of a ravine, probably fell," he interrupted.

"Remi," she replied sternly.

He shrugged again.

"You're not telling me something," she said, her instincts unsettled.

Remy put his hand on the hilt of his sword. "I'm

insulating you. I think we've got someone screwing things up, but I don't know who. If you go around asking too many questions, it could lead to even more disorder and distrust. Anyway, you have plenty to deal with. The water pumps broke this morning. I think it was sabotage."

Christina sighed. "Ever get that feeling like the whole sky is just going to come falling down?"

"Lately, a lot."

Every minute of the four days Christina had been back in Kar'm had served to grind her down even further. There were arguments around every corner. While she loved Remy dearly, it was clear that she shouldn't have left him in charge. He was an odd mix of stubborn bear and cuddly cub, vigorously supporting the people he liked and dodging those he didn't.

Her days were filled with people asking her if they could speak to her for a moment, and she was always being called away to solve supposed thefts or acts of sabotage. People were seeing ghosts all about, and their worst natures were taking over. Despite their best efforts, she and her leadership team couldn't figure out where it was coming from.

She was thankful that Tee, Elly and Mounira had made themselves scarce. The last thing she wanted to do was take her frustration out on the kids in a moment of weakness. She'd given Tee access to her secure underground laboratory, and was happy to see the kid regularly passing the guards and heading downstairs. She'd seen Mounira outside learning to fight. Her mechanical arm was quickly becoming a real part of her.

Christina stopped herself from knocking on the lab's door, realizing that it was hanging on to the frame for dear life.

Canny was crouched in the middle of his blown apart lab, searching for something. He was surrounded by pieces of tables and chairs, and chunks of metal were stuck in the ceiling, each of the stone walls and even the floor. Shreds of burnt paper were everywhere.

"It's gone," he said, standing and rubbing his eyes. His bald head had spots of soot, and his spectacles sat crooked on his face. He glared at Christina, his brown eyes filled with pain and anguish. "The formula notes I had, the entire plan for what we do next to make a rocket-pack... it's all burnt up. It doesn't matter anyway, it didn't work. This was a huge waste of time. I should not have tried. It was a stupid idea, thinking we could fly. You put that idea in my head. You shouldn't have done that," he said, his shoulders slumped.

Christina tried to approach him but he backed away. "You had a setback."

"There's no way to create something that can make a person fly," he muttered, shaking his head. "There's no way, do you understand? Friends of mine are dead because of this. Because of *you*. You fed my hopes, and look what that got me."

"The Fare's airships are real," said Christina, her voice firm and steady. "We need—"

"I don't care!"

"Stop yelling! Why is everyone yelling all the time? I'm not deaf. Canny, you had a setback, that's all."

"No, we're done," he replied, gazing about at the wreckage. "I'm *done*. No more of this." He pointed at various scraps.

"What is everybody's problem around here lately? You've only been at this for, what, three weeks? It's not like you to give up. I believe in you," she said.

He lowered his head, his eyes peeking out at her. "But *I* don't believe in *you*."

Christina was taken aback. "What's that supposed to mean?"

"You've been more focused on the children of foreigners than with what's been happening here. You were gone, you left us, only to dump a crippled girl here, and leave us again! Now you're back, and for four days, *for four days* I haven't seen you *once*. If I'm working on such an important invention, then I'd assume you'd make the time to come and see what was happening. But you didn't."

"Canny, look—"

"No, you look! For too long you've been playing fast

and loose with our ways. You've been letting in anyone claiming to be an Abominator, no matter where they came from. You even let in that Enderian idiot, Henry Blair. He's not even Enderian, he's obviously from Inglea! You let a man who is an obvious liar into our community, into our *home*." He took a breath and shook his head. "The kid, Alex, that he brought with him? He's not even his nephew. These little things, they were cracks in the armor of our society. Now we've got real-world problems digging their fingers into those cracks and leaving us bare and naked. All because you wanted to play mommy."

Christina ground her teeth. "You're on a fine edge, Canny. I recommend you back the yig off."

"No," he said, pointing sharply at her. "How long are you going to be here this time? Just long enough to see things start to boil over, and then you'll run away with your children?"

Rubbing her thumbs over her fists, Christina tried to steady herself. "I've had enough of this. When did you get so tribal? Maybe you'd see what Blair had to offer if you didn't block him at every opportunity. I heard you and your little friends have bullied anyone even considering helping that man."

"Little friends? Is that what we are to you now, little people?" asked Canny, his face red, his eyes burning.

Christina took another deep breath. She'd led these people for a long time, and Canny always seem to represent the everyman. His opinions were rarely offside, and arguing with him was, in a way, arguing with everyone. He was well respected, and despite his introverted nature, was always at their social events. "What's got you scared, Canny? This isn't you," she asked.

"You were our rock," he said, rubbing his hands together. "But for the past several months, you've been distracted and there are consequences. How could you leave Remy in charge? Remy? The man couldn't even answer questions about whether or not we were suddenly supporting the Tub because of the bombings. *Supporting the Tub?* How much of an idiot do you have to be to not immediately answer *no, we're remaining neutral as we always have*. You bringing those kids here has only made things worse."

Christina hung her head, her short blond hair hiding her closed eyes. "Can we back up? Where are we with the flying ideas?"

He gestured about the lab. "It's over. It's a good thing that we *aren't* siding with the Tub, because it means this weird new non-Pieman Fare group has no reason to ever pay us a visit. And thus we don't need to fly. Let the rest of the world worry about the airships, it's not our problem."

"That's ignorant," said Christina sharply.

"No, that's reality. It's cold and mean and real. I'm

going to have everything, including the new prototypes, thrown out. Tomorrow, I'm going to clean my lab and work on something that actually matters."

She stood there, blankly.

"Please, Christina, we need you to do your job. You're supposed to be leading us, so lead. Stop playing with children."

She wished she hadn't lost her whirly-bird, or that she had shared it rather than having kept it secret. With slumped shoulders, she turned and left.

Several minutes later, a short, pony-tailed man walked in. "How did it go? Did you say everything we discussed?"

"I did," said Canny. "I think I went too far, though. She's a good person. I honestly don't think all of this is her fault."

"Hey, don't do that. Don't bring this on you. You did the right thing. She needed to be taken down a notch. All high and mighty, who does she think she is, the queen?"

Canny winced. "She's not like that."

"No, you just don't see her like that, but trust me, she is. I saw it from the moment I stepped foot in this place six months ago. If we hadn't become such fast friends, I'd have left on her account. Don't worry, little brother. Soon she'll be gone, and none of this will matter."

CHAPTER TWELVE
Max'ed Out

Franklin cursed once again as a quill fumbled out of his shaking hands. Trying to rescue it, he knocked a bottle of ink to the floor. "Tee, I will make you *pay* for this," he growled as he crumpled up the large sheet of paper and threw it in the massive pile he'd created behind him. His jacket, vest, socks and shoes were somewhere in the pile as well.

At first, the language and terms used on the plans seemed to decipher themselves right before his eyes. But then everything stopped. At each four hour interval, marked by Simon checking up on him, Franklin's confidence eroded even further. He could feel his deadline rapidly approaching.

He pulled out a pocket watch from his grey pants pocket and swallowed hard. There was only half an hour left. Twenty eight fleeting minutes, to be precise. As doubt and fear started to run circles in his mind, he got up to walk around the study again. He ran his fingers along the books in the endless stream of bookcases.

Imitating Ruffo, he said, "Come on Franky, you're a smart kid. Come on, focus." Then, pretending to be Stefano, he continued, "Yeah. What you need, kid, is a kick in the bottom—" He stopped. "He'd never say bottom. Probably bum? I don't know. Doesn't matter, this isn't helping." He hated the feeling of impending doom. His heart was racing and his whole body was sweaty.

He stared at Simon's locked inner-office door. It was tall and white, with ornate carvings that made it look like a door within a door. The fake outer door looked huge, and he felt small.

He rolled his shoulders and gazed at the floor. "What have I done?" His leg spasmed as if adding its own two cents. He dragged himself back to the workbench and sat down on the stool. Reluctantly, he stared at the giant sheet of design plans. Sighing heavily, he said, "I just wanted to be great. Like Klaus. Like Tee's going to be." He ran his fingers through his sweaty hair. "I don't want to be a nobody... I don't want to be like father. I just want to have that sweet taste of—"

Franklin stopped himself and slid off the stool. There was a thought on the edge of his mind, something teetering back and forth. "Sweet... sweet..." he glanced back and forth between his notes and the plans. "*Sweet...* wait, those vials and bottles in Klaus' lab... Hmm, this..." he said stabbing at one of the sheets, "this is about a chemical reaction! It isn't the design of a real machine, this is just Klaus explaining how the chemicals work together. He just... he *thinks* in terms of machines."

Franklin quickly laid the plans on the floor, then carefully stood up on the workbench and looked at them all together. His eyes went wild and an excited grin grew across his face. "It's... it's *got* to be." Hopping down, he tapped a part of the page. "This is about sugar. It's a solution and... yig, why does he have it? It's... it's got to be a catalyst. Of course, it allows the reaction to happen at room temperature, and that provides the energy to the cart when you hold the handles. Yig! I solved it!"

Just then, he heard the study door open and the familiar voice of the high conventioneer. "Time's up, Watt," said Simon.

"I solved it!" screamed Franklin triumphantly, jumping up and down. "I solved it! Solved it, *solved it!*"

Simon's footfalls stopped. Franklin waited expectantly, but after several seconds, he went looking for Simon.

He found the high conventioneer staring at the floor, thinking. He was tapping his foot as he worked through something.

"Sir?" asked Franklin, unable to read the man.

Simon was dressed in black and grey scholarly robes, a white, high-collar shirt and dark pants. His hair was neat and washed, but his face looked drained. He glanced up at Franklin. "You have thirty seconds. What was the answer?"

"It's, ah…" Franklin felt a lump in his throat, and his body exploded in sweat. "Ah…"

Simon whipped out a pocket watch and shook his head. "Twenty seconds."

"It's sugar. A… a type of sugar, I think. The sheets didn't make sense because they aren't for a real machine —they're just the way that Klaus represented a chemical reaction. It's how he thinks."

The pocket watch returned to its home and Simon glared at the boy. He shook his head in disappointment. "Of course it is. How could I have been so blind? It's obvious. Completely obvious." He turned to leave.

Franklin was confused. "Where are you going? Don't you want hear the rest?"

"I'll be back later. Alfrida will be in shortly to take you to your room. Get cleaned up. Show up this afternoon only if you want to learn what it means to be a conventioneer. Work will be intense, but rewarding. And I'll arrange for you to see your father. That is, unless you don't want to change the world?"

A giddy excitement spread throughout Franklin's body. Just as Simon was about to go out of view, he remembered. "What about my money?" he dared to ask.

Simon turned on his heel. "Where are the steam engine plans?"

Franklin twiddled his fingers nervously.

Maxwell Watt gazed at the floor surrounding his comfortable, high-backed chair. For the past several months, the chair, more than the rest of the two floor townhouse, had been his home. For a gilded cage, he couldn't complain. Furthermore, if he were honest with himself, the limited amount of interaction with the outside world was greatly appreciated.

He glanced around at the piles of papers and books he'd amassed. As quickly as one was removed, it seemed like there were two to take its place. There was barely any wooden floor showing within three feet of the chair. Some of the piles were items of personal interest, others solutions to some of the fun little puzzles that Simon St. Malo had sent his way. "Hmm, I should probably send some of those books back," he muttered to himself. "I can't imagine they'll let me keep ordering them from the royal library infinitum."

When he'd first arrived, he'd been unable to think about anything but the safety of his son, Franklin. Every time he was interrogated, he'd ask about his son and then shortly after, pass out. Finally, one day Simon had shown up with a letter from a spy in Herve. After reading the letter, Maxwell had thanked him and to his surprise, Simon had moved him immediately into his current accommodations. He'd even apologized to Maxwell for his ill treatment and told him he'd been unaware of what had been going on.

Maxwell had become so comfortable that when some

of the other inventors had asked him to join them in making escape plans, he'd ignored them. Instead, he prefered to continue working on the puzzles Simon provided or reading. He thought it a shame that the others weren't seeing that Simon was actually a much better man than they'd given him credit for. He was certain that when the political winds died down, Simon would release him without question or harm.

Maxwell carefully exchanged what was in his lap for a pile closest to the right side of his chair. Masterfully, he managed to avoid disturbing any other piles or spilling the sizable stack of papers he was trying to put down. "Let's see, when's this one due?" He scanned the sheet, finding the due date already circled twice. "That's, what... in two days?" He glanced at the calendar on the wall, almost lost amidst dozens of tacked up papers. Well, might as well get started. Doesn't look like that much of a problem to solve."

Wiggling himself comfortably into place, Maxwell took a fresh pencil to chew on from the set that had been provided that morning. He was going to have to find out how to get some when he got home, as they were far better than the quills he was used to working with. Just as he started to tap into the part of his imagination where he did his best thinking, there was a knock at the door.

Maxwell glared at the dark brown door. Grumbling, he wormed his way through his piles and put his work down. "You people always find the perfect time to interrupt me. What is it you want now?" he muttered.

He smoothed his thin, light-brown hair and adjusted his glasses. With everything now ready, he opened the door. His mouth fell open in shock.

"Hello, Father," said Franklin, with a half-smile.

"Wha... wha—what?" he stammered.

"Watt, actually," replied Franklin smugly. "Have you already forgotten?"

"Is this for real?" Maxwell asked, glancing up and down the corridor, surprised to see no guards about. "You're by yourself? Are you really here, or have I lost my marbles?"

Franklin bit his cheek for a moment before replying. "I can't speak to the marbles, Father, but it *is* me. In the flesh. Might I come in?" He'd rarely seen his father so undone.

Maxwell rubbed his hands together. "You being here can only mean one thing—we're escaping! Wow, I hadn't expected that. Mind you, I did send you to Nikolas Klaus. That old madman, I knew I could count on him! So, are we off?"

The contrast to how Tee and her family worked couldn't have been more stark for Franklin. His father was being classically Ingleash, focusing on the important points of the moment first, afterwards they'd likely share a social moment of concern. He wanted to convince himself that it was clearly superior to the mushy Frelish ways, but he couldn't. He felt disappointment in his father, at his selfish thoughts. *Why isn't he more concerned with me?* Franklin wondered. "What? Escaping? No," he replied.

"But the lack of guards, I mean, we could make a break for it. We could be back home by autumn."

Franklin pointed. "They're just at the end of the corridor. They know I'm here. They let me in."

"Oh," replied Maxwell, his giddy excitement deflated.

"I've been granted permission to see you," said Franklin. "That's something, isn't it?"

Maxwell worked himself up to a decisive nod, finally bringing his gaze up from the floor to look at his son. He smiled and tapped his son on the arm. "It's good to see you."

Franklin hated to admit it, but he appreciated the sentiment, even if it felt like an after-thought. "It's good to see you too, Father."

Maxwell stepped aside and let him in. Franklin looked at the chair and the small kitchenette to its left, the stairs behind it that likely lead up to a bedroom. "This isn't the dungeon prison that I expected to find you in."

"Yes, well," said Maxwell, glancing about, "A cage is a cage, but I do have to say that this one has some respectable amenities, ordering any book from their royal library being my favorite. Puzzles come second. Simon sends them, I think. Innocuous little puzzles to keep one's mind agile. Very considerate, really.

"There's a great deal of professional courtesy at play. I suppose it only makes sense, from one master inventor to another. Regardless of our affiliations, at the end of the day, are we not part of the same brotherhood? I think all of this has really changed my views on Simon, as a person. Yes, he's working with a bunch of people whom I believe to be evil, but the man is... well, decent."

Franklin raised an eyebrow. "It almost sounds as if you like it here."

Maxwell put his hands on his hips and lost his words for a moment. "Um, well... a man adapts, I suppose. Still, I miss the cat, and going to the pub."

"The cat died two years ago, and you *never* go to the pub," replied Franklin, annoyed.

Scratching his head, Maxwell glanced about in thought. "She died?"

"Yes, Father," answered Franklin.

"Well, that's a shame. But the pub... I admit it's rare, but I had the freedom of choosing whether or not I went, and... well, I miss making that decision," he said thoughtfully. "I miss that. I do. Tea?"

"Why not," replied Franklin. As his hand started to spasm, he quickly hid it behind him.

After getting the kettle on, he gave his son a long look. "You've let your hair grow. Hmm. It's fine, just in need of a little trim maybe."

"*Actually*, Father, I'm letting it grow. I'm thinking a philosopher's pony tail might look sporting," said Franklin stiffly.

"Oh," replied Maxwell. "Well, you aren't the little boy I sent into the world on an adventure anymore, are you? I think it's a most reasonable decision, a most reasonable one. Why, I tried to have one once. It didn't work out, but I applaud your spirit! Yes, go after it." His expression looked disconnected and guilty.

"I wasn't a little boy when I left home," said Franklin, irritated. "I think... I don't think you've seen me as I really am for some time, to be honest." He lowered his gaze to the floor, bothered by the truth of what he'd just said.

"Yes, well... a hazard of the profession, I suppose." Maxwell glanced about pensively. "You should have a look at this heat ring, a marvelous little thing." He took the kettle off of the red glowing coil. "It, and all the lanterns, are powered by gas from the ground."

"Oh," said Franklin, looking at the piles on the floor.

Maxwell poured the tea into a pot, placed the leaves in after counting to five, and then decided to ask the big question on his mind. "Did you... um... did you manage to get the plans to Nikolas?"

Franklin's face hardened above tense shoulders. "I made it all the way to Minette. I met Klaus, his granddaughter and some others. But the plans... no. I hid them just before I was kidnapped by agents of the Ginger Lady."

Maxwell waited and then laughed. "Oh, you had me going! The mythical Ginger Lady. You are a cheeky monkey," he said, giving his son a playful punch.

Staring down his father's antics, Franklin said, "No, actually, she's very real. She has three cruel henchmen she refers to as her children. Twisted, demented red cloaked monsters. It took every ounce of genius and determination I had to escape them."

Patting Franklin's arm, Maxwell said, "But... but you're here now, you're safe. That's all that matters. We're together."

Franklin looked over his shoulder at the door, thinking. "Oh, I remembered something. I owe you an apology."

Maxwell finished preparing the second cup for tea and smiled. "Oh? What for?"

A relaxed smile broke out across Franklin's face for the first time. "I should never have given you a hard time about managing money. It's quite the tricky business, it turns out. I had to work for a couple of months just to be able to afford to cross over to Freland. Though I'd honestly thought I had been rather thrifty with my money, I still spent too liberally for my means. Penny wise, pound foolish, maybe? I got robbed a number of times after getting paid for my dirty hours of work. I learned a lot about being alone and having no money. I didn't like it much."

They chuckled together. "Yes, well, I've heard it said not even the destitute enjoy being poor." Maxwell gave his son an affection tap on the arm. "I appreciate you saying that. You're becoming quite the man, Franklin. I am sorry you had to learn some lessons of life the hard way. I'm proud of you, look at where you've gotten."

Franklin smiled stiffly, his eyes confused. What would have once felt like a warm complement now made him uneasy. He gazed about the room again, cringing at the state of everything. "It feels like it's been a million years since we were home, with you burning that letter from Klaus, and whatnot." He accepted the cup of tea and gave it a sniff. "Is that citrus in the perfume?"

"It is," replied Maxwell gleefully. "Lovely brew. They call it Baron Brown. Or is that the other one? Anyway, come, let's sit you down... oh, let me find you something to sit on. I've never had company before. I think there's a stool upstairs. Back in two shakes of a lamb's tail." He returned moments later holding a simple wooden foot stool.

Franklin put his cup on the counter with two hands, hiding another tremor. Something about one of the piles had caught his attention. He crouched down to examine it in detail, and then the one beside it. He looked up at the drawings pinned to the wall to the right of the high-backed chair. "What are these?"

"Those are the puzzles I mentioned," said Maxwell proudly. "The wall has my favorite solutions. Simon sends them to keep us—the inventors in residence here—thinking."

Franklin raised an eyebrow. "In residence?"

"Well, we aren't *prisoners*," scoffed Maxwell. "Yes, our movements are restrained, but I think it has more to do with the times. And the puzzles, I believe they really are a professional courtesy, like I mentioned. Even the greatest minds need a whetstone of problems to stay sharp."

Tapping a particular drawing on the wall, Franklin said, "Have you sent him the solution for this one yet?"

"Which one?" Maxwell adjusted his spectacles and leaned in for a look. "Hmm, about a month ago, I think. Yes, there in the opposite corner of the due date is the submission date. Right now I'm working the one right by your feet, the one with the arcing lines."

Franklin bent down and picked up the drawing. After analyzing its contents and muttering to himself, he rubbed his face. He put the paper back down, and chuckled darkly. He ran his eyes over every drawing on the wall and atop the piles, soaking them in.

Maxwell gestured for his son to sit on the stool. "We can talk about these puzzles and problems later. I hope they'll give you a room beside mine, or maybe move me up to something a little bigger and let us share. That'd be nice, at least until we can go home. Now, you must tell me what Klaus is like."

Franklin stared at his father in cold disbelief. He backed up slightly, shaking his head. "You don't see it, do you?" he asked.

"See what?" asked Maxwell, standing beside his son and looking for something out of place.

Putting his hands behind his back, Franklin raised his chin and said, "All of it. What you're *actually* doing here. You think Simon's been courteous? That he's just being an upstanding fellow inventor?"

"Well, he has. What's wrong with that? The world should be more civilized," defended Maxwell.

Franklin clenched his fists tightly. "You're an idiot. Look at it. *Truly* look at it, all of it! The man has outsmarted you into giving him the steam engine plans piece by *bloody* piece!"

Maxwell laughed nervously. "What? Never. You're just tired, not thinking clearly."

Glaring at his father, Franklin shook his head in disbelief. "Tired? I'm not five years old, Father."

"I know, you're fifteen."

"*Actually*, Father," said Franklin, twitching, "you seem to have forgotten that my birthday was yesterday. I was wondering if I was going to have to point it out."

"No, I'm sure I—" he glanced about, trying to find a calendar. "I'm sure I'd—"

"You're just lost in your own world," said Franklin.

"Do you really want to know about your hero, the *great* Nikolas Klaus? He was *mocking* you, Father. While he helped nudge you in the direction of putting together your cute little invention, *he* had inventions like a rocket cart. I saw it fly through the air with my own eyes. He was so far ahead of you that you were a bug to his boot."

Maxwell's face went red. "That's impossible. You've misunderstood something. You should have more respect. Nikolas—"

"I saw it! You're a *fool*," barked Franklin. "You're a stupid, blind old fool."

"Now, you will watch your tone!" said Maxwell, grabbing Franklin's arm.

Franklin scoffed and shook off his father's grasp. "*Please*. That didn't work *before* you sent me on your pointless errand. You should be careful I don't leave you battered and broken."

"How *dare* you? You're my son and you will—"

"And I will *nothing!*" shouted Franklin, seething. "The trip was good for me. It showed me that I can, that I *must* become so much more than I would at your side, in your shadow. You just breed failure around you."

"What are you talking about? How… how—how dare you?" stammered Maxwell.

Franklin gestured to the mess surrounding them. "I don't know how you did it, but this place already has your stink of defeat and meekness. You've been sitting here, thinking life is simple and good, and instead you've been taken advantage of as the fool that you are," he hesitated before speaking again, with his harshest words yet. "For the first time, I understand why mother left you."

Maxwell slapped Franklin. "You have no right!"

"You think me wrong? Then look. Those diagrams, they are all parts of the boiler." Franklin pulled two sheets off the wall. "These are how the pistons are held." He picked up one from the floor. "This one is part of the steam inlet mechanism. You've been giving it all to him in pieces, willfully! They didn't need to torture you, they just had to give you a nice chair and a pot of tea. Some man of conviction you turned out to be."

Maxwell went white and staggered, putting a hand on the wall to steady himself. "You're... you're wrong. You're just angry and you're just... just... seeing things." He stopped and stared in horror at the truth. Franklin was right. He'd fallen right into Simon's trap. Maxwell remembered sensing something *off* along the way, but he'd so desperately wanted to believe things were better than they really were, that the world wasn't mean and nasty and conniving. So he'd easily been played for the naive fool he was.

Franklin laughed. "YES I'm angry. How many times did I listen when you told me to be humble, that I had to accept when someone else won? You claimed I just needed to try harder, that it would build my character.

Here's the *real* life lesson, Father; only the strong survive. If I follow your lead, I'm going to wind up being a fool with nothing, wondering why everyone around me is achieving their dreams and seeing my inventions stolen from me. I will not end up being a worthless idiot." He straightened his coat. "No wonder Simon offered me this visit. He knew I'd see my instincts were right."

"What are you talking about?" Maxwell's forehead was covered in sweat.

"I'm going to work for... no, *with* him."

"The man's a monster!" exclaimed Maxwell.

Franklin laughed at his father. "Make up your mind, is he a saint or a monster? He can't be both."

Maxwell stared at the papers, scared. The truth was terrifyingly obvious. He mentally put the images together in his head, grasping for something to redeem himself with. "Ah! He won't be able to piece everything together, because he doesn't have... oh, wait... Anyway, there's still time for the Tub—"

"There *is* no Tub anymore. I was there when they captured Anna Kundle Maucher, yet another arrogant idiot. I saw Klaus' house burn to the ground. I've joined the winning side, and all of this, this ability to just take what they need through nothing more than sheer genius, is what I want to do. That's why I gave Simon the location of the steam engine plans. This is my path to changing history."

Maxwell stumbled into his chair, kicking over piles, sick to his stomach. "Please, tell me you're kidding. This is all a horrible, twisted joke. I forgive you. Please, you can't be... Do you have any idea what you've done?" he whispered, his heart pounding.

Franklin stared in disbelief at his father. "What *I've* done?" He waved at the drawings. "Apparently, all I've done is found a way to make some coin on something you were just about to finish giving him for free."

"Son, you don't understand. There was more than just the engine on those plans."

He ignored his father's remarks and continued on his rant. "I listened to you, and what did it get me? It got me humiliated and shocked by a little girl, so badly that I can't even hold a cup of tea properly anymore!" yelled Franklin, picking up his tea cup off the counter and throwing it against the wall.

"Son, please... this has all gone so badly," whispered Maxwell sorrowfully.

Franklin paced about and then stopped, another dark chuckle finding its way out. "Do you have any idea how I got here? I convinced two trained thugs to listen to me, not only because I was smarter than them, but because I was able to drop one of them to the ground with a single blow. Do you know how I got these clothes? I beat street gamblers at their own game. Do you know how I am standing right here? Because I figured out, in a day, what

Simon St. Malo himself couldn't solve after nearly two weeks. I will find a way to be great, and nothing, not even you, is going to stop me."

Maxwell's head drooped. "You can't do this. I didn't know what I was doing, but you, Franklin, you can't. You don't understand what these people are trying to do."

"Actually, I think I have a remarkably good idea." Franklin stepped into the hallway, tugged on his shirt sleeves, and straightened his vest and coat. "We won't talk again for a long, long time. But I will see that you make it home to Inglea. We won't be needing your services anymore."

As he stormed out of the building, Ruffo and Stefano flanked him silently for a quarter of a mile.

"Where we going?" asked Stefano, realizing they were starting to walk in a circle.

Franklin stopped and gazed about at the early evening lights coming from the town down the hill. "I... I don't know. I've got a thousand crowns from St. Malo on me. I'm mentioning this because I'm splitting it evenly with the two of you."

"No, you aren't," said Ruffo, cracking his knuckles.

"That's right, that's not the way it's going to work," added Stefano.

"Oh?" Franklin glanced between them nervously.

"The boss always gets a double share. Half for you, half split between us."

Franklin was surprised. "Really?"

"Rules are rules," said Ruffo. "But seriously, you got a thousand crowns? That's... that's like double what LeLoup was going to get."

Franklin tapped his breast pocket. "It's a thousand, and its in paper. I told you guys I'd take care of you, right?"

"You did," answered Ruffo, truly impressed.

"So, what do you do with that type of money?" asked Franklin, looking at the town.

"Just follow our lead, Franky. We've got this," said Stefano, putting his arm around the lad. "And don't worry, we ain't going to have you waking up in some garbage heap or nothing. You're the boss, and the boss has to be respected, always."

"Yeah, Franky, we got your back," added Ruffo.

CHAPTER THIRTEEN

WITHOUT REGRET

Amami slowed the King's-Horse down to a stop and glanced about as she dismounted. "We should be safe to stay here overnight."

"Are you sure?" he asked. "This old farm house is a bit creepy looking."

"I have stayed here many times. It used to be our uncle's," replied Amami, completing her ritual of shutting down the mechanical horse.

The old house looked very much worse for wear. The field around it that had once been brimming with vegetables was now overgrown with weeds.

"Have I been here before?" asked Richy hesitantly.

Amami stopped and thought. "I... I do not believe so. I had been here several times before you were born. You met our uncle once, when he came up to visit us. After you were taken, and father died—"

"How did he die?"

Steeling herself, she answered, "When you were being taken, father shot Marcus Pieman, and one of the men shot our father. He died a week later of infection." She stared at the ground. "His name was Everett."

Richy couldn't explain the well of emotion he was feeling. He didn't remember the man. "What's... What's our last name?"

Amami stared at him, confused. "How do you not know? Do you know anything about who you are?"

Turning away from her, he said, "The only thing I know is someone thought my name was Hotaru."

Her eyebrows went up. "Yes, the Hotaru! That's why you were taken," replied Amami. "So, you remember that."

"I don't know what it means."

"But..." she stopped, frustrated. She wished she could shake him and bring everything back. "Do you remember the nickname I gave you, Dragon?"

He shook his head.

"You called me Fox."

Richy offered a smile.

"I've used that name everywhere I go," she said, smiling back. She took a saddle bag of supplies off the horse and started to head for the house. "In the morning, we head home to visit mother." As she reached the door, she realized Richy hadn't moved. "Riichi?"

He was standing there, staring at the ground.

She put down her bag and walked back over to him, confused. "Come."

He shook his head. "I can't abandon my friends. Bakon and Egelina-Marie were captured by the Lady in Red. I have to find them and help them. It feels like I haven't spoken to Tee and Elly in years. They're probably worried about me. I can't imagine what my parents are feeling."

"Your parents?"

Richy sat down on the ground under the rising moon and gestured to the space beside him.

Amami looked at him and then at the house. With a gentle nod, she sat down and listened as he explained the life he'd lived. As the evening wore on, they built a fire and talked, never making it into the house.

"The sun's coming up already," said Richy, rubbing his eyes. "I can't believe we talked the whole night."

Amami reached for her saddlebag, thinking. She couldn't believe the life he'd had. "I understand now what these other people mean to you. But I have to share with you that the last time I last saw mother she was trying to waste herself away. She has been burdened with shame and regret since you were taken."

Richy thought through the story Amami had shared. "There's one piece that I don't understand. She built the Hotaru, so why didn't they give me back?"

"That is a question for Mother," replied Amami, standing. "Where will you have us go? To your friends or to see Mother?"

Amami's hands shook as she took off her gauntlets and hung them on the back hooks of her King's-Horse. She felt its heart-panel, and, satisfied, stared at the small family home. She was deeply conflicted between wanting to find mother dead, and finding her alive. She looked at Richy and felt her fears melt away as he stared in wonder at what had once been an oasis in the mountain desert.

Small amounts of bamboo grew here and there. Richy walked up to one of the rusted tubes that stuck out of the ground. "This... this used to be a... a fountain, didn't it?" He turned to Amami, who smiled and nodded. Richy glanced around and then focused on the door. Dusting off his hands, he got up and carefully made his way to it, with Amami right behind him.

As he reached to push the door open, Amami took his hand and pulled him back. Ever the protective big sister, she stepped into the room first, closing the door behind her.

To her surprise, there in the corner was her mother. She held a bowl of cold soup in her lap, and was staring at the mountains. "I'm glad you are back, Amami."

"Mom?" she replied, her lip quivering, her brow furrowed. "I thought you'd be dead."

Her fragile arm shaking, Tsuruko put the bowl on the floor, some of it spilling out. She smiled weakly. "I could not pass from this life with how things were between us. Your father's spirit would have been angry at me for eternity, and I would wish that on no one."

Amami quickly took off her weapons and lay them in a perfect line. She then shuffled over to her mother's side. "There is no need for us to fight," she replied happily. "I found him."

Her mother stared in disbelief.

"Riichi, come in," said Amami in Frelish. She turned to her mother. "He only speaks Frelish right now. I will teach him everything."

As the door opened, Tsuruko's heart raced. With his yellow hood cloak surrounding him brilliantly, Richy slowly looked up at the old woman. "Riichi?" She stared in disbelief at Amami, her Frelish rusty. "How?"

"Mom?" asked Richy, his eyes welling up.

"Ye—" Tsuruko stopped suddenly, her eyes filled with fear. The moment she had been wishing for had arrived, but now she was willing to do anything to stop it. She grabbed Amami's arm and held out her other hand as her body trembled and then started to shake violently. Richy rushed over and took her hand.

"Mom?" yelled Amami, crying. "What's happening?"

"It's a… a stroke," said Richy, remembering the first time he'd seen one years ago. "She's dying."

The old woman struggled against her final moments. "I'm so—sorry, Am…" Her body shook ever even more violently. "Riichi… love you. So big…" And then everything stopped.

Silently, they worked for hours laying their mother to rest beside their father. "They always loved staring at the Eastern Mountains," said Amami, her voice high and tight with grief. She gently took her little brother's hand.

"They are beautiful," he said, staring at them. "She waited for me, didn't she?"

Amami nodded. "But now we are alone."

Richy shook his head. "No, now you become a part of my family. We need to save them."

"I know some people who can help."

CHAPTER FOURTEEN

THE ROCKET AND THE PACK

"Wake up time, Elly. Come on, time to get up," said Tee shaking the mound of blankets.

"Go away, Mounira. You sound tired, go back to bed and let me sleep," moaned a buried voice. An arm came out and attempted to swat the world. "Didn't you promise you'd stop waking me up?"

"Mounira might have, but I'd never agree to such a thing," said Tee, a touch of light-heartedness in her voice.

Elly poked her head out and stared at Tee with one eye. "Why are *you* waking me at this *most unholy hour*, as the Abbott would say?"

Tee put her fingers into Elly's half-empty water glass on the bedside table and sprinkled water in her face. "There, it's holy. Rise and shine time. No more hiding here with books and pretending to be crippled. You've got fight training this morning. We've already been here two weeks, no more doing nothing."

Rubbing her eyes and yawning, Elly fired back, "And I suppose taking apart the shock-sticks and studying them was nothing?"

Tee stared at her, missing her banter cue entirely.

Elly sat up. While Tee had been letting her get away with less and less lately, she'd been trying to push Tee back to *her* old self, as well. "You know, I should kill you for scheduling training so early."

"That... that would violate our no dying rule. Not allowed," replied Tee, a small smile showing up.

"Well," replied Elly, "what about a good old fashion bludgeoning? Or I *could* kill you, then make something to bring you back?"

"That'd be abusing the rule," said Tee, smiling.

Elly smiled back at her. "How are you doing?" she asked, stretching.

The smile grew. "I've learned about something."

"What kind of something?" asked Elly, intrigued.

"One word. Rocket-pack."

"Isn't that two words?" asked Elly, rubbing sleepy junk from her eyes.

"Hmm? Maybe. Probably has a hyphen in it, all the great things do."

"Really?" replied Elly. "I suppose you got a letter from the department of imaginary words, did you? I'm sure rocket and pack don't naturally go together."

Tee shrugged. "It's pretty cool," she said with an odd twist to her grin.

Elly studied her carefully and then snapped her fingers. "There's a boy in this somewhere."

"What?" said Tee, blushing. "No. Don't be silly."

"Really? Why don't I believe you?" asked Elly.

Tee frowned. "Well, not exactly. Listen, they'd been working on a thing like the rocket-cart that Mounira and Christina had used to fly into the air, but it failed. They wanted it as a way to defend against airships that someone apparently has. Someone worse than the Piemans."

"Woo," replied Elly. "That's serious."

"There were people arguing that it was a waste of time and resources, then a couple of people died. Everyone was very hush hush about it, but I stumbled on a few things, and, well… I think we can do it."

"Wait, back up. What's an airship?" asked Elly.

"The way I heard it, it's something like a boat attached to two giant air balloons. There are sails for catching the wind to maneuver, and they drop bombs from the sky," answered Tee.

Elly face tensed. "This is a real thing we need to be worried about now?"

Tee walked over and opened the curtains. "Apparently. There were people working on it, but then the lab blew up just after we got here."

"Why didn't we hear about it?" asked Elly.

Tee shrugged. "People are weird around here. From what I'm gathering, this isn't normal. Anyway, you know what they did with all of their research?"

"What?" asked Elly, thinking through several possibilities.

"Threw it out. All of it."

Elly was shocked. "But, don't they need this thing? Did someone *make* them do that?"

Shaking her head, Tee replied, "I don't know. But something feels wrong. Alex helped me salvage a bunch of it, including some notebooks that weren't destroyed and two partial prototypes, slightly worn."

"Alex?" said Elly, with a smirk. "Details!"

Tee broke into a smile. "It's not like that."

"Of course not, never, no. Details!" repeated Elly.

"Fourteen, dark skinned, a lot darker than Mounira. Says he's from Endera. He might be, I don't know. His name's Alexander Mozhaysky. Sounds Enderian to me."

"All I know is that those people dress well, have sharp accents and really dark skin."

"That's him," replied Tee. "He wears this neat long coat with a high collar shirt and a cute—" Tee stopped herself.

"See, right there. Got you. He's good looking too, I figure," said Elly.

Tee looked away. "Maybe. *Anyway*, we've got a plan. You, me, Mounira and Alex are going to get this thing working. From what I can gather, the mistakes they made in the design are obvious."

"To you," pointed out Elly.

"Alex, too," replied Tee. "There's a lot of chemistry to this, as well. The propellant they were working on... I can't explain it. It feels wrong. What do you think? Want to see if we can make something fly?"

Elly nodded. "If we aren't chasing after people trying to kill us, the least we could do is try to blow ourselves up."

They looked at each other and smiled. It was feeling a bit more like old times. "Does it remind you of the tea on the roof?"

"A little," replied Elly. "I can't believe our parents let us do that when we were little kids."

"Well, they didn't... not really," said Tee.

"True."

Tee smiled. "By the way... I'd like you to be in charge of this. I just..."

Elly was surprised, but nodded immediately. "You make that piece of your Grandpapa to carry around, and I'll get this done."

"I'll still run interference and everything," said Tee. "If we need any."

"Of course," replied Elly.

Tee was relieved. "So, meet us downstairs in Christina's lab after you've had the stuffing kicked out of you."

"Oh, right. Fighting class," said Elly, burying her head in pillows.

"Excuse me, my name is Mounira Benida de—" she said, stepping into the room.

Without so much as a glance away from his workbench, the man replied, "I know who you are. Before you even try to say my name—I can't imagine how badly a Southerner would butcher it—just call me Douglas. And not *Doug*, as so many of them do. You like to just appear out of nowhere, don't you?"

Douglas was one of the prominent scientists of Kar'm, often given nearly impossible problems and then left alone to solve them. He was known among the people for a few mostly harmless explosions, and he hated them all the more for it. Little people with little minds and big fears, he'd often say.

He was precise, methodical and careful. He was dressed with a brown coat, green vest and a cream shirt buttoned up to the top. His spectacles were of his own invention, with multiple lenses on hinges and arms, allowing him whatever magnification he needed with the flick of a finger.

Mounira glanced about nervously. His lab was the biggest she'd seen in Kar'm, except for Christina's. The room was very much like the man; almost oppressively neat, every book in its place on bookshelves, every pile preciously stacked, every drawing or picture on the wall perfectly level and evenly spaced.

She hadn't run into someone as sharp and rude as Douglas yet in Kar'm, but she'd heard rumors. As he turned to look at her, she wondered. "Do you not like me because I'm from the Southern Kingdoms, or is it just... me?"

"You left out the option to choose that monstrosity on your back, that abomination of an arm." He stopped himself. "It reminds me of Stein and his way of thinking, that all parts of a man can be replaced with just the right ingenuity. That man disturbs me."

"Oh," said Mounira. "Well, I can take it off," she said, showing the leather straps under her vest that held it in place.

"I don't care," he turned back to his detailed work. "I don't care about it, you or anyone else. The fact that you are of dark skin and a Southerner rather than an Enderian or from Dery or anywhere else doesn't make me hate you any more. I hate everyone equally."

"Well, as long as you don't play favorites," replied Mounira, wondering what to say next.

To her surprise, he laughed. He put down his instruments and gave Mounira a real look. "I heard that you ask a lot of questions, to the point of making some people want to run screaming, but they said nothing of your wit. I like wit."

Mounira smiled. "I heard they would not let you work on the rocket-pack project, is that true?" She tried to peek at what he'd been working at, only to be pushed away.

"No, they did not," he replied drily. He rubbed the bridge of his nose. "What is it you want, little Luis?"

"Do I look like a drowned boy to you?" she asked sharply.

"No, not particularly," he replied with a grin.

"Then I ask that you call me by my name, Mounira."

"How about I call you Jill, it's easier," he said, leaning against his workbench.

"No," insisted Mounira.

His grin grew. He folded his arms and stared at her in wonder. Like many people in Kar'm, he had resented the presence of the Yellow Hoods, but his motivations were different. Without her strong sense of vision and drive, he'd seen Canny's brother muscle his way in and start pushing people around. He'd quickly found himself isolated. "What do you want... Mounira?"

She reached into a pocket of her yellow cloak and handed him a notebook. "Open it to the bookmark, please. We'd like you to tell us if we're right about the fuel."

"*We* is the Yellow Hoods, I suppose?" he asked, taking

it from her.

She shrugged. "If I say nothing, you don't have to lie."

He smiled. "Smart girl."

"We think we can make the rocket-pack work."

Douglas tapped the notebook against his hand. "This project was shut down, you know. You're not supposed to be working on this. It blew up Canny's lab, killed a few people. If he or anyone else heard that you were—"

"We are being careful," replied Mounira.

"Hmm," wondered Douglas. "Are you trying to show Canny up?"

"No," answered Mounira. "We just think maybe someone helped it fail. We want to see if, with the help of the right people, it can work."

"And I'm one of those *right people?*" he asked.

She nodded.

"Hmm. Who told you to come to me?" he asked, curious.

Mounira shrugged.

"Smart girl," he replied, grinning again. "You know, the early prototypes they had were better than the one that blew up, it's a shame they threw them out." He studied her expression. "But you have those? Huh. I'm impressed."

"We're building a new one."

Douglas pulled on his ear in thought. "You must have Henry Blair and his nephew involved if you're doing that. There's no one else with the mechanical and metal skills to make a body that's light but strong enough. He's involved? Hmm. He's a clever kid. So, all of you are working together with those of us on the outside of the project. Impressive. Tee must be leading this."

"Elly, actually."

"Really? Hmm," he noted her slip but decided not to make a point about it. "Why do you think you will be any more successful? Assuming it wasn't sabotage."

Mounira smiled excitedly. "We're thinking of the new rocket-pack more like a firecracker. Something that throws you into the air for a short while, rather than—"

"Yes! Rather than something that sustains flight. It's like a... a mythical jump, like the stories of old heroes, where they were able to jump, almost run on the wind for a moment, before plunging back down to Eorth! The mechanics and propellant needs are completely different and much simpler to deal with this way." He tapped the closed notebook against the workbench. "I'll go through what you have here and will let you know my first thoughts. You have to keep this completely secret. Things are bad enough as it is. The last thing I need is Canny's brother coming and screaming at me any more. I swear I'll throttle the man. He's poison." Douglas flipped through several pages of the notebook. "Come back in a few hours, I should have some initial thoughts for you."

"Thank you, Anciano Douglas."

"Actually, it's Douglasino. Armando Francisco Douglasino. These people," he glared about, "they just can't pronounce things. But I can hear it in your melodic speech. Give it a try."

"Thank you, Anciano Douglasino."

He stared at her, a hint of a smile revealing itself. "You have a fierceness to you. Don't lose that."

<hr />

Mounira barely noticed the nod from the guards as she hurried down the stairs to Christina's lab, where Tee, Alex and Elly were expecting her. "Elly, these are the last of the notes and comments I gathered," she said, pulling them from her cloak and tossing them to her.

"Great," said Elly with a wink and smile. It was hard to remember the little kid that she'd been jealous of. While Mounira still would sometimes lose control and ask a million questions or miss the humor of a moment, Elly would never forget the sight of Mounira streaking through the sky on the rocket-cart. "By the way, did you find out anything about the whirly-bird?"

"Nothing. I never..." Mounira glanced around uncomfortable.

"What is it?" asked Tee.

"Well, her room door was open, so I stepped in and had a quick look." Mounira cringed. "I shouldn't have done that."

Elly nodded in agreement. "I appreciate the thought. The last thing we want is to get Christina angry at us."

"And you and I have searched every part of this lab over the past few weeks, Elly," said Tee, still working with her back to everyone.

"Maybe she didn't make it here," said Alex bluntly, his sharp Endearian accent standing out.

"Huh," said Elly. "That's a good point."

"A mystery for another day," said Tee, pushing up her goggles and spinning on her stool to face her friends. "That's everyone's input that we need, right, Elly?"

Elly gazed at the notebook. "It is." She glanced at Tee, smiling. She hadn't really expected Tee to be completely comfortable with letting her run the project, but she was.

Alex pointed at some papers on Tee's workbench. "My latest changes, did you have a look?"

She reached for them and handed them over. "I think they're really good. I made a few notes; just thoughts, really. I think you nailed this, Alex."

"Nailed?"

"Oh, sorry," she said, remembering that Frelish wasn't his first language. "I think you got it right." A flirty smile escaped.

Alex's face lit up. "Oh! Tha—thank you."

Mounira rolled her eyes, muttering to herself about teenagers.

"Okay, Tee, you're done," said Elly, going through her

mental checklist. "You can work on your armband. We'll bug you when we need you."

"Hello," said Christina at the door, startling everyone. "So the lab that I said you could use for your analysis of the shock-sticks and Tee's armband has become a clubhouse, I see." She stepped into the room, her arms folded, studying everyone.

"We can leave," offered Mounira.

Christina offered a stiff smile. "No. I can see that nothing has been touched, save for what I said you could use. And I can understand wanting to be away from the tension upstairs, particularly when you hear people whispering about you Yellow Hoods. All that I ask is that when you continue to treat the space with respect, and please, no one else other than you four. Tee, Elly, I'm holding you guys responsible."

"Understood," replied Elly.

"Which brings me to the question of *what* you're doing." Her expression hardened. "You've been snooping around for information on the rocket-pack, asking a lot of questions. I thought it was a curiosity for a few days, but it's gone on too long. I went to check where the prototypes had been dumped, and found them missing. I don't know where you have it, but it's pretty clear to me what's going on. Did you think no one would notice? This is the last thing I need you guys doing. Never mind the political headache you're giving me, I don't want you blowing yourselves apart. Canny is one of my best guys, and he... he couldn't get it to work. That's the end of it. If these Skyfallers, as they're called, show up, we'll just need to find another way of dealing with them. So to be clear, I need you to stop what you're doing. Understood?"

They all stared at her. Christina had dark circles under her eyes, and her face looked thinner. Her head hung lower than normal, and her shoulders were rolled forward. There was an air of disappointment in her voice, but it wasn't directed at them—it was like she'd let herself down. They could all sense that she didn't like saying what she was having to say.

Tee turned around and pulled down her goggles. "Can we talk, just you and me?" she asked.

Elly hid her smile and ushered everyone else out with her. She closed the door after them.

"You and I both know that there was something wrong surrounding the rocket-pack. We're just trying to figure out what it was so that we don't get blown to pieces."

Christina rubbed her eyes. "Did I ever *say* that the Skyfallers were coming here? No. I just wanted to be prepared. The vault across the hall holds over two hundred years of inventions and scientific ideas, many of which didn't work. Failure in this area is nothing new."

Tee hesitated. She glanced at the little painting of her Grandmama she'd taken from Nikolas' downstairs study just before they'd fled his house two months ago. "Are you sure this was really a failure? I promise we won't blow ourselves up."

"No. I need you guys to stop with the rocket-pack stuff, Tee." Christina walked over to the workbenches and glanced at the papers. "Your armband is coming along, focus on that. There's a lot of fear going around. Some people seem to think we have spies everywhere, trying to tear us apart."

She looked up at Christina, her eyes steely and her face showing she was ready for a battle. "I understand. You don't want me poking around in your world? Okay, fine. Then tell me what's happening in mine."

Christina frowned and folded her arms. "What's that supposed to mean?"

"You think I don't know my father lied to me?" said Tee, stepping off her stool. "Elly picked up on it, too."

"He didn't lie to you," said Christina, definitively.

Tee shook her head, she wasn't buying it. "I *know* my parents, my dad especially. He didn't have to say something that wasn't true, I can hear the holes. I also caught a glimpse of you walking out of the Abbott's office with him, so I know he spoke to you."

Christina thought for a minute. "I don't believe you saw us. You're fishing for something."

"Are you or are you not hiding something?" asked Tee.

"Look," said Christina sharply.

"No, you look," rebuffed Tee. "You're feeling guilty about having gotten tangled up with us, I can see that. I'm sure part of you wishes you never came out to get us, but from what I can gather, you'd been missing before you ever met us. There's no sign of you doing your whirly-bird work here, so I'm guessing you were spending time somewhere else. Wouldn't it help if we could get the rocket-pack working? We could show that we add some value around here. And if those airships show up, then we'd have a fighting chance."

Christina pushed her short hair over one ear, and then the other. "Those are big ifs. Few people even know that Kar'm is anything more than ancient ruins. And even if they did, how do you sneak a behemoth like that up on us? We'll see it coming days in advance. We'd figure out how to drop them out of the sky."

"I think you're wrong," said Tee.

"I'm the leader, and I understand the risk we're taking. Right now, what I need is for you guys to stay out of the politics and out of everyone's way. One day you can solve the rocket-pack problem."

Tee nodded slowly, staring at the floor until Christina left. Putting her goggles back on, she whispered, "That day is today."

CHAPTER FIFTEEN

Emotional Chasm

Caterina couldn't smile at the early morning sun, despite the wonderful smells coming in from the outdoor kitchen and the gardens. She stood on her stone balcony, three floors up, gazing down on the part of the world where her word was solemn and final.

Her years of maneuvering had paid off. She'd fought hard to convince the heirless king, and all of his advisors, that she should be Regent. Some had required more brutal convincing than others. She dispelled the pressure to either hand over the reins of rule to a parliament, as was becoming fashion, or to a distant cousin of the king's. Her decision to annex the neighboring kingdom of Elizabetina had caught many off-guard, and allowed her to silence many of her critics during the confusion.

She stared in the mirror at the fading blotches on her face, a modest smile of victory showing. The attempted poisoning had scared her, forced her back into her red-hooded cocoon. But, like the influence of her father from beyond the grave, it was losing its grip on her with each passing victory: rallying the royals in opposition to the Piemans, starting the civil wars in the Southern Kingdoms, and, most recently, capturing Marcus Pieman himself. Seeing Marcus carted away in irons had brought her an immense sense of pride. It had also opened her eyes to the possibility of being able to create her *own* destiny, far from the path her father had forced her to take. Soon, Marcus would be hung, and the grand game would be over. She wished she could just kill him, as he was notorious for turning things to his advantage, but the political ramifications would shake apart her fragile empire.

Stepping back out to the balcony, she watched with pride as an experimental design of Skyfaller lifted out of its rail-raft container and up into the sky. Using the railways to overcome their short flight times had been a stroke of accidental genius, and one that had allowed her to wipe out the royals of Myke by surprise. By first ruling the rails, she'd set everything up for ruling the skies.

Her thoughts drifted to Bakon, and she stared at the grass below. For years, she'd secretly wanted nothing more than to be with her sons, but that was a long time ago. She needed to rid herself of the sense of hesitation she felt inside.

Egelina-Marie's eyes opened to the sound of intense

knocking somewhere downstairs. She was surprised to see Bakon awake, reading. Their bedroom made up the entire second floor. The main floor had a simple kitchenette and sitting room. The door was guarded at all times, but occasionally they'd been allowed to walk the grounds. "I must be dreaming, because I've never seen you read."

Putting down the book, he gave her a fake stern look. "Don't worry, I'm not. I'm just tracing all the letters with my eyes."

"Oh, okay. Wait, that sounds *remarkably* like reading to me," she replied, sitting up. "And here I thought I'd caught myself a mindless ruffian."

The knock came again.

Glancing at the stairs, then back at Bakon, Egelina-Marie wondered if she was imagining the sound, as Bakon seemed to be ignoring it.

Bakon tapped the book thoughtfully. "You know, a ruffian has to keep up to date on the latest ruffian news. What's happening with the latest clubs? Is oak still recommended against travelers or is it now birch?" Eg started to laugh. "What about the best lines for robbing people? Is it rude to be quick and to the point, or is it more effective?"

"Stop," she snorted, immediately embarrassed.

"Heh heh. Don't get excited, it's just a book of fairy-tales." He tapped it again, his face revealing the ripples of thoughts deep down. "My mother used to read this one to me."

The knock came again, along with some words they couldn't understand.

"I better get that," he said heading downstairs.

Eg reached over and picked up the book. "The Three Piggies and Other Fine Tales, by Martha Gooz." She tried to imagine Caterina, the Lady in Red, the Regent of New Staaten, once upon a time sitting with a little Bakon on her lap, reading a book. It was far easier to imagine him with their own little ones one day, reading to them.

Bakon opened the front door.

"Finally," said an annoyed bald man in a red cloak.

"Another guy with gold embroidery," said Bakon. "You must be important, to someone."

The man chewed on his lip and then offered a smooth as silk smile.

"Good morning, Beldon. My name is Lord Silskin. May I come in?" he asked.

Bakon didn't move or say a word.

Silskin grimaced. "Do you prefer Bakon? My apologies. Do you know that you have your father's, face but your mother's eyes? Remarkable. So very similar, and yet different, from your sister."

Bakon kept his stony expression but stepped out of the way to allow Silskin entry. He could tell the man was an experienced talker, and wouldn't have been surprised if he was lying to manipulate him. Bakon figured if he'd ever had a sister, he'd know. "Come in... like we have a choice."

"Oh, you do, just... not one you'd likely care to exercise, my good man." Silskin turned and smiled at Egelina-Marie as she descended the stairs. "Good morning, Mademoiselle Archambault. I'm sorry you haven't received any attention since arriving, but I hope you've enjoyed the accommodations?"

"Yes," she said glancing at Bakon. "They were... a bit of a surprise, I have to admit. I thought we'd be in a prison cell."

Silskin laughed. "Why? You aren't our prisoners. You are guests. I mean, Bakon Maurice himself is here."

Bakon shared a surprise glance with Egelina-Marie. "The door's guarded and we can't go wherever we want."

"Yes, well, we are all restricted guests of some form or another. We can't have people stumbling off the edges of castle walls because of construction, and whatnot. We have a lot going on at the moment, and we can't be too careful."

"Now, please tell me, have you been escorted out and about to tour the grounds over the past week?"

Bakon nodded. "It's a nice enough place."

"Good, good, I'm glad to hear it," said Silskin, his head held high. "Now, if you'd come with me, we can walk and talk. Her royal highness, Regent Catherine, is very busy at the moment."

"Wait," said Bakon, confused. "But my mother's name is Caterina."

"Ah. There's a story there, I'm sure. Anyway, shall we stroll? It's a lovely day," said Silskin. His tone was compelling as he gestured to the door as if it was the way things needed to be.

"Um, okay," said Egelina-Marie, reaching for her boots. "Bakon?"

He glanced at her and nodded. She could tell there was a lot going on. The gears were moving behind his eyes. Neither of them had a plan yet.

"Oh, one thing I'd like to mention," said Silskin, his tone switching to reveal he was far from simply a glorified host. "The Regent has appreciated that you have not tried to escape, as am I. Though you are our guests, the guards and soldiers are under orders to kill you, outright and without hesitation, if you attempt it. It's not personal, but there's a standard to be maintained, and we cannot have *any* exceptions."

A chill ran through Eg and Bakon.

Leaving the building and entering the northern gardens, Silskin started pointing out various breeds of rare flowers.

Bakon was struggling holding on to his sanity, the level of boredom beyond anything he had ever experienced or imagined. He marveled at Egelina-Marie's ability to nod and smile, unaware that her mind was hundreds of miles away.

Silskin picked up yet another flower and Bakon snapped. "I appreciate the tour or lesson or whatever it is you think you're doing, but what do you want to talk about? It can't be this. Please, tell me it isn't," said Bakon.

Egelina-Marie hid her smile, proud that Bakon hadn't just outright punched the guy, as much as she wanted him to.

"Fair enough. I can see you're a direct man, which doesn't surprise me. Your mother is very much the same way. I need you to tell me what you know about the Piemans, the Fare and the Tub."

Egelina-Marie squeezed Bakon's hand before he said anything. Keeping his eyes on Silskin, Bakon replied, "We live in a small mountain town you've probably never heard of—"

"Minette? Please. We know full well where Minette is, as well as its origins and history. Of all towns to try and claim to be from and thus be ignorant of the Tub, that is not one of them. You see, I know the Archambault family, as I was the one that recommended your grandfather move there, Mademoiselle. As for you," he said turning to Bakon, "I hear you were raised by the Klaus family. Nikolas Klaus would have been involved with many important people over the years. Please, continue."

Bakon started walking again, needing time to think.

"Beldon?" asked Silskin.

"Bakon," corrected Eg. "His name is Bakon Cochon."

Silskin tried to hide his disgust. "Very well. Bakon?" he asked.

Egelina-Marie glanced around, picking out the guards who were keeping an eye on them from a distance. "Scratch that," she muttered to herself, dropping one escape idea.

Slowing down, Bakon said, "The Klauses raised my brothers and I until we moved into a house we built as teens. They then just… kept an eye on us. I beat people up for a living." He noticed how the statement no longer felt true. "All I know about Nikolas Klaus is that he's a nice old man."

Silskin soaked in Bakon's expression, his body language, word choice and tone. He nodded as he processed it. "What about these Yellow Hoods I've heard about?"

"The kids? You're concerned about a bunch of teenage kids running around with capes?" asked Egelina-Marie.

Glancing at Bakon and seeing the same expression, Silskin replied, "No, I suppose not. One last question; what do you know about Franklin Watt?"

Bakon shrugged. "I don't know, I met the kid for about two seconds. Seemed okay."

Silskin pulled out a pocket-watch and considered the

time. "Okay, well. Have a good stay. I'll speak to you again soon, I'm sure."

Egelina-Marie leaned in and asked Bakon, "Do you trust your mother?"

Rubbing his fledgling beard, Bakon scanned and stopped as he noticed something floating in the sky. "No."

Mister Jenny rubbed his hands together nervously as he stood ready to knock on the marble framed white doors to the Regent's attending room. He'd been one of many to learn recently that the Regent Caterina was also the Lady in Red. It connected a disturbing number of dots, and was obvious afterwards. Silskin had clearly known, as there was no sign of surprise, and Jenny couldn't believe how masterful the man was at keeping cards so close to his chest.

"Are you ready, sir?" asked Alfrida's twin, Zelda. She was wearing a white jacket, shirt and pants, decorated with red at the shoulders and elbows.

He shook his head.

"Whenever you're ready," she replied, returning to her statue-like pose.

Jenny took off the old leather backpack and double checked its contents. In it, he caught a glimpse of the original letter he'd received from Caterina directly. He'd found it waiting for him on his kitchen table, neatly propped up and no signs of anyone having come or gone. At first, he'd suspected it was really from Silskin, and that he'd returned to his paranoid ways. It had been years since Silskin had laid a loyalty trap for him, but he never put it past the man.

He checked his red jerkin was clean and straightened his criss-crossing leather straps. Zelda had taken his pistols and put them aside. The two guards that stood ten feet away were well armed and trained, but he knew Zelda was the real guard. Despite her soft tones and graceful gestures, he could read one of his own kind. Her beauty was a natural distractor. She reminded him of Richelle.

"I'm ready now," he said nodding to convince himself.

The double doors opened. Zelda entered and then motioned for him to follow. Once he'd crossed the threshold, she closed the doors behind him.

Mister Jenny gazed about the grand room. The walls were decorated with blue and silver marble, brilliantly reflecting the light pouring in from the open balcony doors. Paintings lay sitting on the floor, leaning against the walls; clearly a change of mood was about. In the middle of the room was a large, round glass table. On it was a bounty of fresh fruit and bread, wine and water. Sitting at one of the four chairs around the table was his host, her red hood down.

"I present to you her royal highness, Regent Caterina Maurice," said Zelda.

"Your majesty," said Mister Jenny, bowing his head. "Your request has been completed."

"Good. I'd heard rumor to that effect. Please, Mister Jenny, join me." She then looked at Zelda. "You can leave us." She caught the look of concern on Zelda's face. "You may stay in the adjoining study, if you want."

"Thank you, your majesty." Zelda shuffled off and closed the study door at the opposite end of the room.

"I can see surprise on your face, Mister Jenny. There have been a few attempts on my life recently, one where I had requested Zelda to leave, and she pretended to. She made it to my side at a critical moment, shall we say. She and her sister are devoted, and I've learned to be a bit more appreciative of their concern." She motioned for him to sit.

He put his worn leather backpack on the ground and made himself comfortable in one of the fine wooden chairs. He ran his rough fingers along the glass table top. He'd never seen anything like it. He resisted the childish urge to move his hand underneath it.

"Did you eliminate all of them?" she asked, taking a loud bite of a bright red apple.

"Yes," he replied, glancing up at her and then politely moving his eyes away. "And there were no witnesses. I put the evidence in place, as you requested. Everything should point to the Piemans, if someone investigates."

"Someone will." She leaned in. "How certain are you that there is no trail to be followed back here?"

Mister Jenny felt the heat of her gaze. "There is always the possibility of something, your majesty. But none that I am aware of." He paused, wondering for a moment about the scar that ran down the side of her face. "I'm only concerned about the people who saw me leave here to carry out the act, as well as return."

"You came in through the underground entrance, as I requested?" she asked.

"Yes."

"Then you have nothing to worry about," she said, smiling. "Mister Jenny, you should relax. You've accomplished something the Tub and many others tried and failed at. You've eliminated the entire Council of the Fare at once. No successors, no ability to recover—they are finally gone." *Finally. Now I truly have my Freedom*, she thought. "It's not every day a man gets to single-handedly topple an ancient order. My path will no longer be interfered with by small minds."

He glanced at her, his face showing questions he wasn't sure he should ask. He'd never heard of the Council of the Fare before her request. He'd learned on mission that they also called themselves the One True Fare, a way to differentiate from the group who followed the Piemans. He didn't understand the politics, and knew he was better off staying out of it. He was, however, getting tired of being a weapon in their silent war.

She stared out the open balcony doors at the hot summer day. "Does Silskin know anything?" she asked, taking another bite of her apple.

He stroked his mustache and thought through his answer carefully. "No, at least not yet. I wouldn't be surprised if he learns of what happened soon. He always seems to find out."

"He does, doesn't he? The rumors will travel quickly to him, but they have little power over him other than being a distraction. He'll need to see it himself." She drew a circle on the glass table with her finger. "Piecing together the truth will take him time, and by then, it shouldn't matter." She noticed the backpack. "Is that everything I asked for?"

Mister Jenny followed her glance and nodded. He picked it up with both hands and put it in his lap. "Everything from the meeting rooms, including the red leather satchel. It was right where you said it would be. I didn't open any of it."

A smile of delight crossed her face as she took the items from him and placed them on the glass table. She carefully opened the leather satchel and double checked it held all of the signing seals. "You are one of the few men I have met with a well-earned reputation that doesn't do you enough credit, Mister Jenny." She looked at him, wondering. "People are most vulnerable when they think themselves victorious, are they not? Was the Council celebrating Pieman's capture? Was there an air of having won the grand game?"

"Somewhat, yes, your majesty," he replied. He knew it was better not to share what he'd really seen or heard. The job was done, and in the end, she could rewrite history however she wanted.

A loud popping sound came from outside, drawing their gaze to the experimental Skyfaller. It was listing to one side, apparently being bogged down by a series of broken pipes. They could hear the captain cursing and ordering his small crew about.

She stood and smiled. "That is the sound of progress, Mister Jenny. We cannot afford to lose our focus or determination, especially when we think we've won. The finish line is always truly a mile away from where we last thought it was."

Mister Jenny was glued to his seat, staring at the sky in disbelief. "What is that?"

"Haven't you seen them before?" she asked. "Have a good look. That is the future. My new design has sails and piping along the sides that allows it to catch the wind, and cool the water." She glanced at the grandfather clock across the room. "This one has lasted longer than the other prototypes. It's the third generation, and soon will be gracing the sky everywhere. The greatest change to this generation is that it will only take us weeks to build one. The first one took years. Progress is an amazing thing."

He was speechless. He'd heard rumors of air balloons with a ship's body, but it was far too simplistic for what he was witnessing move through the air. Even lurching to one side, it had an air of limitless power.

Caterina continued, "For years, there were whispers that the Piemans had a secret weapon called the Hotaru. It was a fabled airship, one that he had hidden just behind the next ridge somewhere. Yet we never saw one, nor were any spies ever able to find a scrap of evidence it existed. Marcus Pieman, more than anyone else, knows how to create an insidious idea. He didn't have to build airships, he just had to make people *think* that he had them, and by never talking about them, he only strengthened the rumors."

"But now, the world thinks that Marcus Pieman's airships have been attacking, and soon they will look at my beauties as the saviors. Our only line of defense against the terror of the Piemans. My little children, my floating beauties, they will bring me the world."

"Oh," said Mister Jenny as something clicked. "The reason for the delegates, and the attacks under Pieman's name… you need them to revoke his rights as a head of state."

She smiled and nodded.

He stopped himself from asking anything else, realizing there was no long-term good that could come from his curiosity.

"You're a smart man, Mister Jenny. Loyal, too. I've done my research on you, from the days before you were a trainer for the Piemans to now. However, I need a new level of loyalty from you from here on out." She went through the papers Jenny had given her and found what she was looking for. "Your leash is cut," she said, handing it to him.

As he read the sheet, his cheeks went red, his eyes welled up. "The location of your daughter, her name and everything. I can't imagine what it must have been like when you were forced out of the Piemans' service by my father's heavy-handed tactic of killing your wife and claiming to have killed your daughter. And then, what it must have been like to know that your daughter was alive, but you could never find her."

Jenny kept re-reading the letter and then checking the date in the upper corner was recent. "I don't know what to say," he said, his throat tight with emotion.

"You don't need to say anything. Just understand that I take care of my own, Mister Jenny. Are you with me?"

He looked at her and nodded.

"Might I suggest you take no action on this matter until everything is settled? It will definitely draw Silskin's attention, if not that of others."

He nodded again, unable to find words.

"Speaking of distracting matters, I have another request for you, Mister Jenny," said Caterina, staring at the Skyfaller as it regained control. She paused and tapped the glass.

"Yes, your majesty?" asked Mister Jenny, surprised at the look of indecision on her face.

She glanced at him before returning her gaze to the airship. "Have you heard we have two guests? Bakon Cochon and a woman named Egelina-Marie Archambault?"

He shook his head. "I've only just returned, your majesty."

"We discovered them in the company of Abeland Pieman. While they…" she stopped, momentarily losing confidence in what she was about to say. She scanned the gardens below, and was disappointed not to find Bakon and Egelina-Marie walking about. "I want you to watch them on the expedition to Kar'm. If they survive, discover whose side they are on. And if that side isn't ours, I want you to kill them."

Mister Jenny nodded, his brow showing he knew there was something more to it. He bit his tongue rather than ask why she was sending them on a mission, but it was a mystery. She never did that with others whose loyalty she questioned. Clearly, there was something more she wasn't willing to discuss. "Understood, your majesty. Do you want me to contact you after I witness anything, or simply take action?"

She sighed and wondered. She sat down and stared at him. With firm confidence in her eyes, she said, "I've changed my mind. If they survive, kill them. Regardless. My destiny is mine and I can't afford any distractions."

CHAPTER SIXTEEN
AN ORDER OF REDEMPTION

The inn was filled to the brim with soldiers and support personnel, yet again. Gretel and Ray had definitely earned their place, and with Ray's suggestion at raising prices, Emery was able to afford to pay them for their devoted work. He tried not to think of the implications for the world around him, with an endless stream of soldiers, and now dignitaries, coming through. He was exhausted, and feeling like the richest man on a deserted island, wondering why he ever wished for anything other than the peace and quiet he used to complain about.

Emery was too tired to jump when a man gave him a slap on the back and a friendly voice filled his ears. "Need a help in the kitchen? Your staff out there is running a pretty tight ship, but you look like you need a hand."

"William! William Baker!" said Emery, instantly filled with energy. "I'd feared you'd been killed or captured, with what happened in Mineau."

The tall, thin man smiled. "No, but things aren't good. I've got to get back there in a day or two, but needed somewhere to stay. Do you have room? You look like you have a full house."

"Bah, I never give them the good rooms. We'll find you something. Are your wife and daughter here? It's been ages since I've seen the little one."

"Tee's fine, I just saw her in Costello."

"Costello? What's she doing over there?" asked Emery, waving for one of his staff to hold a minute.

"Have you heard of the Yellow Hoods?"

"Hoods..." Emery snapped his fingers. "Yes! There was a group a while back, complaining about them, a month or so ago."

"That's her and her friends," said William with a proud smile.

"Really?" replied Emery. "Just them?"

"Well, they have a bit of help, but it's mostly them."

"Good for her. How's Jennifer?" asked Emery eagerly.

His old friend's expression went more solemn. "Let's talk about that later, okay? Now, what do you need? Someone to chop? Call orders? Put me to work."

As the sun daringly shone its morning light through the open doorway of the inn, Emery slammed some mugs of ale on the table. "Okay, enough cleaning and everything. All of you, come here," he said. "Ray, put those chairs down. They might even fix themselves if you give them half a chance."

Gretel nudged him with her broom. "Hound, he means you."

"Oh," he replied, nodding.

William pulled up a chair and smiled at his old friend. "Since when have you been this busy?" he asked. "That's insane."

"Lately, it's almost every night, for months now. I think everyone within a hundred miles has now worked for me at some point. Few have been as helpful as these two. I had a great young woman helping me keep everything together for a while, Alice. She left on a short trip weeks ago, but never came back.

"The past couple of weeks, I've seen less soldiers and more dignitaries, some with Southern Kingdom colors. I think I even saw someone from Beleza, if you can believe it."

"Are you sure you want us to join you?" asked Gretel.

Emery nodded and gestured. "Please, you guys hold it together. Gretel, Ray, this is my friend William."

"We met through the course of the evening, but it's a pleasure to meet you officially," said Gretel, shaking his hand. She glanced at Ray, who then stuck his hand out as well.

Emery took his mug in both hands and leaned back. "So William, where's Jennifer?"

Picking up his own mug and staring into it, William let his exhaustion quell the emotions that wanted to stir up. "We heard that something was going to happen in Mineau and went to check it out. The city was quickly overwhelmed. The Magistrate was in on it, and more than half the guardsmen turned on Captain Charlebois. When the foreign soldiers arrived, they spared no time in laying waste to the city. They scooped up the survivors and sent them in caravans to Kaban to be sold as slaves."

"That's terrible," said Emery. "What happened to Jennifer?"

"We got separated, and I believe she was taken in one of the caravans." William glanced about the tavern. It was strangely silent after the raucous evening. He scratched his forehead and then continued. "I was hoping to find some allies, but the world seems to be coming apart. We've lost a lot of good people. Do you remember Pierre DeMontagne?"

"No, I'm afraid not," replied Emery.

"Pierre died saving my daughter from a Red Hooded archer," said William.

Emery looked over at Gretel who was going pale. "Are you okay?"

Gretel glanced about nervously.

"She hates stories where something happens to a child," replied the Hound, squeezing her hand back. "How old is your daughter?"

"Thirteen," replied William.

"Thirteen already? How time has flown," said Emery.

"I wish that was the worst of what's happened to Tee lately, but it isn't. I couldn't ask her to come and help me find her mother. Maybe I don't have enough faith in my daughter, but I'm scared what it would break her. Never mind her best friend and what's happened with *her* parents. I'll just need to find another way. It's good to know that she's safe, at least."

"We'll help you," said Gretel, her voice trembling.

William and Emery stared at her in surprise.

"That's nice of you," said William, his hands raised in appreciation. "But you're needed here, and I need warriors."

"We know how to fight," said Ray. "I didn't get these good looks by playing with puppies." His deadpan tone brought everyone to a laugh.

William shook his head. "I can't ask you to do that."

"I'm good with a bow and sword, as well as other weapons," said Gretel. "Please."

Looking at Emery, William asked, "Can you live without them?"

"If it were anyone else, I'd say no. But I do have to ask a favor," said Emery, the edge of his mouth curling up cheekily.

"Anything," replied William.

"If you find that cartographer, Driss of Zouak, punch

him in the face for me, please. I heard last night that everyone is coming here because he put my little inn on a map a year ago." He looked at Ray and Gretel. "Are you sure about this?"

Gretel nodded, holding Ray's hand.

"Well, hopefully Alice returns soon. Otherwise I'm going to close it down and cry in my mountain of money."

William stared at Gretel and Ray. There was something in their eyes that he understood. "Okay, then. Thank you."

CHAPTER SEVENTEEN
A Benjamin, Tee'd Up

"Now," said the booming instructor's voice, cutting through the noise of the courtyard.

Elly's eyes snapped open and scanned about the open-air training room. Immediately she spotted a man and woman charging at her from opposite sides. She blocked the woman's attack with a wooden staff, and then rolled out of the way of the man's club. As she lunged at the man, he grabbed her hand and yanked her across the room, into the path of the woman. Narrowly dodging the attack, Elly yelped and fell to the ground, holding her side.

"Stop," commanded the instructor from the catwalk above. She quickly climbed down and gave Elly a helping hand. "You've been getting better each day. I wanted to push you harder today. How is your side?"

Through gritted teeth, Elly replied, "I'm okay."

"You've gone from reluctant to relentless," replied her

instructor with a smile. The woman was over six feet tall, with straight brown hair done in an elaborate braid. Her skin was dark and her arms were covered in tattoos the likes of which Elly had never seen. Her face was sharp, and her accent similar to Alex's, but not enough for them to think she, too, was Endearian. "Don't be disappointed. You need to stretch that side, get your body to understand what it can and cannot do, so it does not let your mind attempt something it will not do successfully. Go practice your throwing. I'll see you tomorrow."

Elly nodded, rubbing her side.

The instructor glanced about. "Where's Tee? She's supposed to be here now."

"I'll find her for you. It's not like her to miss a morning class."

"Thank you, Elly. I'll work with Mounira in the meantime. She's really become one with that mechanical arm of hers."

Elly noticed Alex sitting on a bench, staring up at the sky. He seemed peaceful, lost in thought. She liked how excited the two of them got sometimes when talking about the rocket-pack. He wasn't intimidated like many of the boys were in Minette, never mind the other girls.

Even in the hot weather, he was dressed with his worn, yet regal blue coat, collared shirt and white pants that went down to his knees. Elly smiled as she got close enough to hear his mutterings. He was always at work on the rocket-pack, as was she. She hoped that he and Richy would get to meet, as she could see them being friends.

Glancing around, she sat down near but not beside Alex. She watched as people went about their morning routine, many of them walking through the courtyard and ignoring the soldiers and others training. "Are you thinking about whether or not you want to add wings again, as you stare at the birds?"

"I'm trying to think like a bird, see where *our* thinking might be wrong," said Alex as he continued his sketching.

"I've been thinking about propellants," said Elly.

Alex stopped, and smiled at some people walking by. "Plural?"

"Yes, I'm thinking we need two different ones. One for ignition, more explosive, and then the other that would burn more steadily," proposed Elly, looking in the opposite direction.

"Hmm," mused Alex. "This idea, I think it is a good one. One to pop and one to push, yes?"

Elly nodded, a hidden smile at him using one of Tee's expressions. "Are you going to show your uncle your new ideas?" she asked.

Alex stared back up at the birds flying over head. "I would have, but he has left."

"Where did he go?"

"I do not know," said Alex shrugging. "I found him packed up and ready to leave. He offered for me to come with him, but I told him no. He warned me against staying, and then left."

"I'm so sorry," said Elly.

Alex's expression showed no real concern. "I know you know he is not really my uncle. I respect that you have not asked or mentioned it. But it does not matter. With you Yellow Hoods, I have purpose, both intellectually and morally. This is where I want to be."

Elly looked at him, nodding. "Indeed." She then had a mischievous thought. "I'd like you to do something for me."

Tee took another thin strip of leather from the stash she'd found and tied some rogue hair up in yet another ponytail. Taking off her goggles, she stared at the armband design drawings pinned to the wall. "Where are you?" Going back and forth between her assembled device on the workbench and her diagrams, she tried to think where the last issue was. "You aren't going to tell me, are you?" She wondered how many times Christina had failed with the whirly-bird before it worked.

She touched the side of the goggles and noticed it was wet. "Leaking again? Already? I'm going to have to really fix this seal later," she muttered as she reached for some wax and tools. A minute later, she was satisfied. She'd found them waiting for her on the workbench one day, an anonymous gift. Apart from being beautiful and ornate, they seemed old. She'd never met something so small and elegant as how it used water and pressure to change the magnification of the goggles' lens.

Looking over the grapple bolt mechanism of her armband, she wondered how her Grandpapa had done it. "Maybe the springs are too tight? Maybe too thick?" She couldn't get it to fire properly. She stopped all of a sudden and stared at the doorway. "Is someone there?" She pulled down her goggles and walked over, peeking into the empty dim, stone corridor. Though lanterns were hung every six feet, they were old and cast a gloomy light. "Hmm, must be nothing." She headed back to her workbench.

A while later, Tee stretched and jumped up and down, trying to reinvigorate herself. Not feeling awake enough, she ran on the spot, holding onto her brown pants that were two sizes too big. "Okay, let's do battle," she said to the armband once again. She fixed her rope belt and her cream blouse. "Ms. Drawings, do you have anything to say?" she asked the wall, widening her stance and studying them. She grabbed one of the things Canny had called a pencil and twirled it in her hand, a habit she was starting to enjoy. She couldn't believe how much easier the pencil was to use than a quill, and with no need for ink. Yet another marvel of Kar'm. "Come on, what am I not seeing?"

"Maybe it's not what you think it is, but something right beside it. Something that's too obvious to see if you stare straight at it," said a voice.

Tee nodded, her mind focused. "Maybe... maybe the bolt's cable isn't threading right." She put the goggles back and prodded around. "Actually, I think I should reinforce this part of the trigger mechanism." She reached to the edge of the workbench and took a small, leather-wrapped metal rod out of a bed of glowing red coals. With surgical precision and a small piece of copper, she fused some parts together. "Now what do you have to say?" she asked the device. "Are you going to work?"

"What is that?" asked the male voice, approaching from behind. "I never feel like you've given me a real answer."

"Huh?" said Tee, spinning around in surprise, knocking her stool over. "Alex? What are you doing here?"

"Um... you didn't know I was here?" he asked. He blushed and looked away as he realized how Tee was dressed. "You're... in pajamas."

"No," replied Tee. She then glanced down and laughed. "Ah... sort of. What are you doing here?"

"Elly sent me."

She shrugged off her embarrassment and looked at Alex. "You can look at me," she said. "Just don't be too scared by the hair."

"It's not proper for a man to—"

"Alex, these are not my pajamas. These are just comfy, that's all."

"Oh," he replied, slowly bringing his gaze up.

"So… how long have you been there?" asked Tee.

Alex scratched his head. "You've been talking to me for a couple of minutes."

"Really? Oh." Tee smiled. After a few seconds, she realized that Alex was just staring at her. "Alex?"

"Yes?" he asked, straightening up, his hands behind his back.

"Elly sent you," prompted Tee.

"Oh! Yes. She mentioned you were missing training this morning, and I should come get you. She said something about it being better coming from a Benjamin. What does that mean?"

Tee went beet red. Many years ago, Tee had had her first crush on a boy named Benjamin. Ever since then, it had become code. They even used it for girls Elly liked, which they felt was a fun secret irony. "It means I'm going to have to kill her."

Alex was surprised. "But… Isn't she your best friend, and didn't you save her life?"

"Yes, well, that was then. Pre-Benjamin." She paused. "I'm kidding. Sorry," she replied.

"Oh," he said, relieved.

"Anyway, I didn't miss training this morning, I just did it earlier. She's just messing with me."

"Um, I thought that was possible, so I confirmed with the instructor," said Alex.

"She's mistaken, then," replied Tee.

He glanced around the room. "There are no windows here. One could lose track of time. Are you aware that it is Thursday?"

"Very funny," said Tee. "I get it. I've been working down here a lot." She smiled at Alex. "I appreciate the concern."

"You have big eyes," he blurted out, going red in the process.

Tee laughed. "Yes well, they *are* twice the size of my head."

Alex stared at the floor. "Um. Just to be clear, it *is* Thursday," he said. "Elly said you've been here since yesterday after training."

"You're kidding, right?" asked Tee, a hint of worry.

"No."

"Wait, the instructor's expecting me?"

Alex nodded. "That's what I've been saying."

"Ah!" yelled Tee, bolting past him.

CHAPTER EIGHTEEN

UNCONVENTIONAL MOMENT

Franklin stretched and glanced with blurry eyes as he awoke. Once again, he'd fallen asleep at his workbench. It was a funny feeling, but one he was getting used to. He rubbed his eyes and scanned about, spotting a trolly with a pot of tea and some toast. He glanced about for Alfrida, who was nowhere to be seen. "She's a ghost, that woman."

It had been an interesting few weeks working side by side with Simon St. Malo, particularly lately. Franklin had learned that Caterina was the one person able to strike fear into Simon. He'd also learned that Simon had retrieved the steam engines plans, but was intentionally not working on them with him, which bothered Franklin immensely.

He stared at the closed main doors to the study and thought of Ruffo and Stefano. The guys were getting bored. Money only held their interest so long. He'd ask them to hang on a bit longer. If the time came when the guys were going to leave, he wasn't sure if he'd actually stay with Simon.

The grand study door opened and Alfrida came in holding a tray of tea and toast and stopped right in front of Franklin's workbench, stunned. He glanced at the trolly and then back at Alfrida. "Um, I haven't touched the first set yet. Sorry."

Alfrida was beside herself. "But, I didn't bring it. I never bring in tea and toast before seven o'clock."

Franklin pulled out the pocket-watch Ruffo and Stefano had bought for him. "It's five past seven," he muttered. He reached over and touched the side of the pot. "It's not piping hot."

"I spent the past half an hour looking for the trolley. No one knew what had happened to it," said Alfrida.

"Half an hour? Well, that gives us a timeline," said Franklin, looking around. "Put the tray down on the table by the fireplace, and wait outside in case our intruder hasn't left yet."

"Should I alert High Conventioneer St. Malo?" she asked.

Franklin thought for a moment. "Not just yet. Maybe this is a practical joke of some form."

Alfrida shook her head. "St. Malo hates practical jokes."

"As do I," mused Franklin, slowly walking through

the maze of bookcases. He stopped, twiddling his fingers. "I'll fetch you if I find anything out of place." He wondered what was afoot. He couldn't imagine that people were actually able to get into the study unannounced. Simon had made a point of sharing with him all the defenses and security measures he had. Yet the evidence was compelling. Suddenly it dawned on him to check the always-locked inner office.

"Closed. But are you locked?" said Franklin, staring at the door. Carefully turning the knob, Franklin opened the door and stepped inside.

Simon's inner office was a bright room, lit by windows that saw out to the garden, and with walls that went up thirty feet to the ceiling. It had a seating area by a fireplace, a dark workbench with ruffled papers on it and a large desk at the far end of the rectangular room. Along one of the walls were dozens upon dozens of pinned papers, like those he'd seen in his father's room. On another were maps and other designs that pulled Franklin to them.

He studied them and then found something of serious interest. "What's a rail-raft?" He carefully removed the paper and studied it. He put it back, and took another. "Rail-rafts... trains. Hold on, what's this?" He removed a third sheet which clicked it all together for him. "This *train* thing... it uses my steam engine." He stared at the floor in disbelief. "Christina was telling the truth? Someone *actually* needs the steam engine for something concrete?" He scanned through the other series of drawings and notes. "So, they want to move whatever a Skyfaller is around by train. Okay, well, that's interesting." He turned and looked at the other wall. "Hmm, what have we here?" He smiled as he pulled a drawing he first thought was pure fantasy until he studied its details. "A Skyfaller is an *airship*. And this one will be powered by the engine? Really. Well, this... Beldon generation of Skyfaller has got my attention, indeed."

He closed his eyes and thought, ignoring his shoulder as it spasmed for a few seconds. "Maybe they built the air balloon ships first, then needed to move them, so they built the rail-rafts. They had to, because they didn't have the engine, and thus the reason for going after father. Ah... this makes sense now. Wow. I can't believe I'm standing in the middle of all of this." He wandered over to a map with finely painted lines. His heart filled with pride and ambition. "These are the rails for the train. They go nearly everywhere. Amazing."

Something caught his eye and he scanned about until he was able to figure out what it was. Some of the papers weren't lined up properly along the wall. He looked at the ones on the opposite wall, they were perfectly straight. "Someone was clever, but not clever enough for me," he said, smiling.

Carefully, Franklin moved over to the desk and found the drawers all slightly open. After checking them, he gently closed them. Turning to look out the window at the back of the office, he noticed the chair was turned toward the window. He spun it around, revealing an envelope on the seat. Glancing at the door first, he picked up the unsealed envelope and lifted the card out.

"Thanks for everything, especially your treachery. See you soon, Abe Pieman," read Franklin aloud. He gently replaced the note. He gazed about, tapping the envelope on the back of his other hand. "He's being set up. Hmm, that's interesting." A sinister idea hit Franklin. Turning his back to the door, he pulled out a hundred crown note from his money pouch and slid it into the envelope. He returned the card to the seat and tucked his shirt back in.

"What are you doing here?" asked a booming voice from the doorway.

Franklin stiffened and turned around, his hands up.

"Franklin Charles David Watt, your Regent asked you a question," said the red hooded figure at the door.

Franklin's eyes focused on the gold embroidery along the edges of the cloak. He'd never met someone who instilled such fear in him. "Who...who..." he stammered.

"I am Regent Caterina Maurice. But relax, I am not accusing you of anything. Alfrida already informed me that you were helping." She pulled back her hood, revealing her scarred face.

Franklin started to bow and then stopped, "I... I don't know what I'm supposed to do... Do I call you 'your majesty'?"

She smiled, instantly relaxing the teen. "Why are you in here?"

Franklin glanced about. "The door was open."

"Open?" she asked, surprised.

He stared at the ground. "Unlocked," he confessed.

She looked him up and down. "I believe you. Tell me what you've found."

Franklin walked her through the papers on the wall that were not aligned. She then noticed the dust where a notebook had been removed, and went through the drawers, disturbed by some of the letters she found.

"And then there was the note on the chair. I'd just seen that when you arrived," said Franklin, pointing. He was sweating profusely.

She picked it up, curious about his nervousness. "I heard a rumor that it wasn't Simon who had figured out the Klaus design plans. That it was you. Is that true?"

Franklin stared at the ground, wondering. Just as she was about to ask him again, he looked up. "Yes. Yes, it is true."

"After I read this, we have much to discuss. I want to know what's *really* been going on."

As Caterina and Franklin walked out of Simon's office, they heard the main door open, and then the unmistakable sound of someone running.

Simon skipped to a stop in front of them. His face was

a mix of rage and fear. "What are you doing here? Why wasn't I told *immediately* about—"

"You always had to play both sides, didn't you, Simon? Ever wanting more attention? It explains a lot," said Caterina.

With a shaking hand, he pointed sharply at her. "*You*, of all people, are trying to play that against me? You? Cat… Caterina."

"Oh," she said playfully, her eyes piercing. "You finally have the courage to say my name? After all these weeks, I wondered if it would ever happen."

Simon's eyes darted around the study. "I demand to know what's happened here."

"You demand? From the Regent?" she asked, smiling politely. "Alfrida, are you there?"

"I am, your majesty," came her voice from somewhere in the maze of bookcases.

"Please send for the royal investigator and some guards of notable size. Don't worry, they're only a safety measure, in case we have a problem. Do we have a problem, *Conventioneer* St. Malo?"

Simon's face went flush. "How dare you, I'm the—"

"*You* have whatever title I see fit, I'm the Regent. If you're cleared of the charges of treason, then your position as High Conventioneer will be restored," said Caterina, tossing the envelope at him. "But I'll tell you this, it doesn't look hopeful."

"What's this?" asked Simon glancing down at the envelope. "A letter of execution?"

"Maybe, but it's not written by my hand," said Caterina.

Simon glared at Franklin. "What is this?" he asked removing the card inside.

"It was on your chair," answered Frankly, his hands shaking. "Some of your papers on the wall had been moved, too. Hard to notice at first, but I could tell."

Caterina quickly added. "Your Neumatic Tube has been used, too. As if someone took the papers, sent them somewhere, had them sent back, and then tried to make everything look like nothing ever happened. Maybe they sent them to our enemies so they could have monks quickly copy them? Or maybe they just needed to read them, to see what we were up to? Interestingly enough, it seems like the person responsible left you a letter, and a tip."

Simon removed the letter and the hundred crown note. "Abeland?" He was mystified. "How could... wait, this isn't his handwriting." Studying some of the loops it hit him. "Richelle! Richelle Pieman must have done this. You have to—"

"I *have* to do nothing," said Caterina, slowly and decisively. "You and I both know what that money means. That's one of Abeland's playful signatures, isn't it? A way to say that the rest of the payment has been sent wherever it was supposed to be sent. It explains now why you didn't kill him. How much did your loyalty cost?"

Franklin turned away from the conversation, his eyes wide with surprise. He couldn't believe the impact of what had been a sudden impulse. He felt his hands tremble. His mind was racing.

"What do you think?" asked Caterina, surprising Franklin.

He stared at her, lost.

"What do you think we should prioritize, in terms of invention? You caught a glimpse of what was going on in Simon's *former* office. What do you think we should be doing?" she asked, hinting that he should repeat part of their private conversation.

Simon wore the desperate expression of a caged animal.

"We should build the steam train, but not the version I saw in there. My father had a limited vision and understanding of it. I can make us one that's ten times better."

Caterina shot a glance back at Simon. "Very well, *Conventioneer Watt*, so it shall be. I'll have you know that suspended *Conventioneer* St. Malo had recommended we go slow and steady, and, moreover, that you wouldn't add any potential value. Prove him wrong, and you'll change the world."

Franklin avoided Simon's burning gaze.

Putting her arm around her new conventioneer, she added, "You may use this study as your own, for now. Alfrida will put you in contact with our army of metal-smiths, advisors and whatever other resources you need. Don't disappoint me."

CHAPTER NINETEEN
SCOUT'S HONOR

While their hooded cloaks kept the heavily falling rain at bay, Amami and Richy's boots were no match for the muddy puddles. As they approached the small town's stone arch entrance, Amami grabbed Richy's arm.

"We need to be really careful here. Don't look anyone in the eyes, and let me do all of the talking," said Amami. She glanced around to make sure no one was paying attention to them.

Richy glanced at the plaque with the town's name. They were in Teuton somewhere, at a town he'd never heard of. "Okay. You look worried, why?"

She was surprised. "You mentioned Marcus Pieman, don't you know who he is—was?"

"Not really," replied Richy.

"He was the president of the country you're in right now, Teuton. With him gone, the parliament has fallen into chaos and civil war. Red Hoods have been seen everywhere. Remember what I told you the other night about them?"

Richy nodded. "Run, stun and lastly, kill them, if need be."

"Yes. They cannot be trusted," she replied, smiling. "I'd prefer if you weren't wearing that cloak, it's very noticeable."

"It's the only one I have, and more than that, it's *who* I am. It makes me feel connected to my friends." As lightning flashed, Richy noticed something about her cloak. He reached out and confirmed it. There was black embroidery on the edges of dark fabric. He looked at her. "Who are you, really?"

"There will be time for that later. Right now we need to find out where your friends are, and the only person who I can trust to help us is here," she answered, leading the way.

Richy nodded and followed. He had no reason to suspect anything, and he knew deep down that she was his sister, no matter what else she might be.

As they drudged through the muddy streets, occasionally getting splashed by horses and carts making their way in the dark afternoon, Richy noticed something. He reached forward and tapped Amami on the shoulder just as she was about to turn down a side-street. "We're being followed."

Taking a deep breath, she reached under her cloak to confirm her weapons were in place and ready. "Charge your...?"

"Shock-sticks, got it," said Richy, fidgeting under his cloak as they continued straight ahead.

"We'll double back in a minute, when there are less people around, or down another side-street," said Amami, thinking of how the town was likely laid out. "Can you climb well?"

"Yes," he said reaching out and touching the brick of the nearest building. "I think I could scale up one. There's enough stuff to run up—"

Both of them stopped in their tracks as an electrified crossbow bolt narrowly shot passed them. They turned and stared at a Red Hood who was reloading a two handed, fat-tubed weapon with another bolt. His partner was yelling at the pedestrians to get lost, firing in the air with his pistol.

"Did he just *shoot* a shock-stick?" asked Richy, panic taking over his face. "Who are these people?"

"Is your cloak bullet-proof?" asked Amami, glancing at the buildings and the confused pedestrians around them.

"I think so," said Richy, his charged shock-sticks firmly in hand.

"Run at the gunman," commanded Amami. "Trust me."

With a nervous gulp, Richy did as ordered. The partner took a shot, which bounced off harmlessly as Richy put everything he had into not slipping on the slick cobblestone road. The Red Hood smiled as his weapon was nearly reloaded. They both could see he'd have a chance to fire before Richy hit him.

Suddenly, Richy felt a weight on his shoulders, and then he watched as Amami flipped over him and kicked the Red Hood square in the chest, knocking him clean over. Richy pivoted and struck the partner with one of his shock-sticks. Out of the corner of his eye he saw Amami hide something back in her cloak as the Red Hood flailed about, blue lightening arching on his body as it did on the partner.

Amami walked over and took the big weapon, slinging it over her shoulder. She then grabbed the coin purse of the Red Hood and threw the coins around, distracting the onlookers.

"You'll like my friend Eg. She's a lot like you," said Richy with a smirk.

—⁓—

The door creaked open and the carcass of the old bell bonked. The old woman at the meat counter hadn't needed the bell to alert her for decades, though for the past few years she'd spent hardly any time at the shop. She closed the book she'd been reading and looked over her spectacles at the two hooded figures.

"So, Amami, you keep company with a Yellow Hood now?" she asked, sitting back in her stool and folding her arms. Her curly grey hair and round face gave her a grandmotherly appearance, but her eyes were sharp and her presence tangible.

Pulling back their hoods, Richy glanced at Amami who shrugged. "How do you—"

"Oh, my!" said the woman standing up. "Come here, child. Come." She gestured to him. Richy approached the counter and the woman grabbed his cheeks and stared at his eyes. "They're blue. True blue as I've ever seen. You found him? You found Riichi?"

Amami nodded.

Richy gently removed the woman's hands from his face. "Who are you?" he asked. "Are you my aunt?"

"No," she replied touching his arm gently. "I knew your parents, and a few years ago, this young lady showed up here. She was in trouble. It was one of her many attempts to find you. I gave her a helping hand and introduced her to some people who could teach her to take better care of herself. When I heard about a blue-eyed boy with a face from over the Eastern Mountains, I sent her a message. And here you are."

"Thank you," said Amami. "I am forever in your debt."

Richy recognized the cane behind her, leaning against the wall. "Where did you get that?"

Glancing over her shoulder at it, she shrugged. "It's an old thing. I've had it for years."

"No, you haven't," replied Richy, reaching into his cloak. "That was Anna Kundle Maucher's. I'd recognize it anywhere. Who are you?"

The old woman's eyebrows arched, as she studied him. "Where are you from?"

"Who are you?" insisted Richy.

"Please, Riichi, she's a friend," said Amami.

Richy glared at the woman. "Madame Maucher led Tee, Elly and me into a trap with the Red Hoods... But you know that already, don't you?" he said, seeing something in her eyes.

"Yes, Anna told me before she died a couple of weeks ago. We escaped when Marcus' palace was destroyed, but she didn't make it far."

"Wait, that means you're the Butcher!" said Richy. "I can't believe it."

"My name is Eleanor DeBoeuf, Senior."

"Then you need to help us find Elly and Tee, and Egelina-Marie and Bakon—"

Eleanor put up her hand, cutting Richy off. "Have you heard of Kar'm?" she asked, looking at him and Amami. They shook their heads. She continued, "We heard a few days ago that Caterina was planning something big for Kar'm, but we aren't sure if we can trust the source. Sam Baker is off trying to finalize support from the one remaining ally we seem to have."

Richy stared at the floor, his sense of duty coming to the forefront. "How do we help?"

"Amami, do you still have your King's-Horse?"

She nodded.

"In the morning, you'll start scouting for the rails and anything interesting going on. I feel we have little time."

CHAPTER TWENTY

THINKING WHAT I'M THINKING

"Oh," said Bakon, as they came over the ridge and saw hundreds of people working below. "I guess I don't need to ask where you're taking us anymore." He dismounted and stared in disbelief. "What is all of that?"

"Those thirty foot wooden platforms with the chairs are rail-rafts. They ride on those metal lines, the rails. Those things in the middle of the platforms are how they move. It's unlike anything I've ever experienced," said the escort soldier, a smile on his face.

"So it's people powered," said Egelina-Marie, surprised.

The soldier beamed with pride. "For now, but I hear they're working on that."

"What is that thing?" asked Egelina-Marie pointing at something that was being pulled into a rail cart. "Is that some kind of air balloon?"

"*That* is a Skyfaller. If we had arrived earlier, you

would have seen it come close, lower its ropes and be slowly pulled onto the cart. They really are something to behold. Monsieur Maurice, you should be quite proud. This will be a legacy with your name on it."

Bakon grumbled.

A very young soldier approached and exchanged salutes with the escort soldier. "Private Jugend will see you to see your seats. Enjoy our first outing. We don't usually have dignitaries on these missions, but I believe it's always best that you get to see what is really happening in the field."

Egelina-Marie glanced at Bakon and then at the escort soldier. "Agreed," she said, trying to sound official but worried she sounded corny. The closer to the rail-raft they got, the more curious Eg became of the chairs. "Why do they have ropes?"

"Because if they didn't, you'd fall off," said Jugend, rolling his eyes.

Eg nodded. "How many rail-rafts are there here? There seem to be three Skyfaller carts and lots of soldiers."

Jugend looked Egelina-Marie and Bakon over. "Ma'am, I don't see any official indications of your rank, so I'm going to have to decline answering that."

Bakon chuckled. "Oh, boy."

"Ma'am? *Ma'am?*" replied Egelina-Marie. "How old are you?"

"Ma'am, I'm just—"

Egelina-Marie stepped forward. "Ma'am!?"

Bakon put a hand on her shoulder, and shook his head.

"How old *are* you, *kid*?" she asked. "Twelve? I bet Richy could babysit this kid."

A distinguished looking lieutenant with a fat face stepped in, dismissing the private. "Mademoiselle Archambault, Monsieur Maurice, if you would please follow me to your seats."

Eg glanced at Bakon, who was thinking. After they were seated and shown how to properly tie themselves in place, she finally leaned over to Bakon. "Are you okay with them calling you by your mother's last name?."

"There's more to this whole Pieman and Maurice thing than we're seeing," replied Bakon.

"True. Maybe I'm just trying to defend you. Why didn't you correct that boy? Calling me ma'am."

Bakon smiled at her. "I didn't realize you needed defending."

"A woman can be strong and still appreciate some chivalry now and then."

Nodding, Bakon replied, "I'll keep that in mind."

For a while, they watched the soldiers make preparations for their departure. Despite having asked along the way, they had no idea where they were headed or what the mission was. All they knew was that it was important.

"I have an idea," said Egelina-Marie. She grabbed the arm of a passing soldier. "Excuse me? Are we leaving just yet?"

The soldier glanced around. "No, Mademoiselle. It's probably... I don't know... another twenty or thirty minutes."

Smiling with her eyes, she said, "Oh. Well, do you mind if Monsieur *Maurice* and I get up and walk about for a bit? All of this is so wonderfully new to us."

"I don't think it will be a problem," he replied. "You'll just need to hurry back to your seats when they blow the whistles. Is that okay, Monsieur Maurice? I hope it doesn't bother you, but I must follow protocol."

Bakon nodded, puffing himself up. "No worries, proceed my boy."

Eg elbowed him as the soldier left. "Don't ham it up too much."

"That was too much? Geez, it was half what I was thinking."

She buried her head in her hands. "What am I going to do with you?"

"Stop them from taking over the world?" offered Bakon.

"Yeah, sounds about right."

CHAPTER TWENTY-ONE
FAMILY MATTERS

Christina tightened her fists as she approached the roar of arguing voices coming from the former royal court chamber. Despite the years, the room had presence, and was only used for the most important meetings. She hated getting yanked, once again, away from an issue that was nearly solved because there was a bigger problem that required her attention. There was an endless stream of bigger issues, and a flooding river of unhappy people.

As she stepped into the room, all eyes turned to her. In all the years that she'd been at Kar'm, first as an Abominator seeking refuge, and then working her way through the leadership, she'd never seen things in such a state. It felt like someone was intentionally taking everything apart, but she nor her inner circle could find any evidence of a plot.

Remy was standing on the elevated platform. His face was flushed with frustration and his arms folded defensively. Christina dragged herself up beside him and scanned the crowd. More than two dozen parts of Kar'm were represented. Everyone was fed up.

"Why's she tapping her pistol?" asked someone. "Is this her new way to keep things under control? Unacceptable!"

Christina glanced down, and stopped the guilty finger from tapping her streaming gun anymore. "Would someone please tell me what this is all about? You've been tearing each other apart for weeks now."

Canny's voice cut through the rest. "You've abandoned us to play mommy with those... those children." His brother was beside him, nodding in profuse agreement.

"You're touching your pistol again," Remy whispered.

Christina scanned around for something she could slam her fist on, but there was nothing. Finally, she erupted, "Stop it! Stop this... this *mob* behavior! You are the most intelligent, inventive people this side of the Eastern Mountains, and look at yourselves. Something clearly has you spooked, and you're falling apart. You're tearing *us* apart." She gazed at the paused faces, many of them glancing at those around them. "The world out there is scary right now, and we need to come together now more than ever before. If everyone takes a bolt from the machine, then no one should be surprised when the whole thing falls apart." She noticed Canny's brother whispering to him. "And if *anyone* says I or anyone saw this coming, they are lying. And if you knew, then shame on you for not bringing it up."

Straightening her brown leather vest, she subconsciously counted her belt pouches and she paced. "We're used to existing solely for the good of progressive thinking, a refuge from the purge of brilliance, a beacon against the age of dark mindedness that has spread."

"It's a nice speech, but the reality is that they are coming for us," said Canny. "Can everyone else feel it? There's something wrong." Many nodded, some looked about nervously.

"That isn't helpful," chastised Christina. "You of all people—"

"I, of all people?" replied Canny, "I told you weeks ago when you visited my lab. Since then, things have only gotten worse. The Piemans and the Tub, they used to leave us alone. And now?"

There was a look in Canny's eye that bothered Christina. She glanced at the faces around him. Something was up, but she couldn't put her finger on it.

"Christina," said Angelina stepping into the room, her voice booming and drawing everyone's attention. "You're needed upstairs, now."

"Excuse me?"

Angelina stared at some of the faces in the room, many of them already not fans of hers. "I wouldn't be here if it was not *critically* important."

"I can't. I can't be pulled once again. We have to—"

"Christina. You have to come up. Trust me," said Angelina.

"She planned this," said a voice.

Canny's brother shook his head. "Typical."

Christina put her back to the crowd and whispered to Remi, "How about you go?"

He shook his head. "You know she wouldn't be here asking for you if it wasn't supremely important."

"Any ideas what it could be?" asked Christina.

"None. Sorry," he replied.

As she took her first step off the platform. The look in Canny's eyes had spread.

"Christina, I need you to come with me," insisted Angelina, stepping in and taking Christina by the elbow.

"Remi?" she said, looking back.

"I've got it, Christina," he said emphasizing his size and pulling on his red chin-beard.

"You didn't have *it* before she walked in, Silskin," barked a voice from the crowd.

Tee finished the trek up the forested hill and glanced back at Kar'm. There was too much activity going on. People were rushing, some packing up, few saying anything. It reminded her of how Elly's dog, Chichi, would whimper before a storm rolled in.

"Hello, Tee," said Alex, looking up as he pulled the camouflage tarps off the two rocket-pack prototypes.

"You know, I'm still surprised no one has found this," said Elly, putting her backpack down.

Mounira shrugged. "No one's looking for it, isn't that how Anciano Klaus hides things?"

Tee smiled and looked back at her friends. "Yeah, he did."

"*Does*. We'll get him back," said Mounira with complete confidence.

Tee nodded. "Grandpapa says that people are often most blind there." She returned her gaze to Kar'm.

Elly looked at Tee's raised shoulders. Putting a hand on her shoulder, she whispered, "Go and work on your armband. It's nearly done, anyway. We're okay here."

"Are you sure?"

"Yes. Now go, we'll be good. I'll let you know what happened, if Mounira doesn't beat me to it," said Elly.

Glancing at the supportive faces, Tee took her cue and left.

"She is okay, is she not?" asked Alex, his voice extra stiff.

Elly had hung around him enough to know that he cared, and she liked that. "She's almost all Tee again, just a couple of things left."

"Christina still doesn't know anything about this, does she?" Elly asked the other two.

"No... but she suspects something. I was almost forced to tell her," answered Mounira.

"Just lie to her," said Alex, frowning. The girls looked at him. "What?"

"You haven't known Mounira long," said Elly.

"I can't lie to Christina." Mounira gazed at Tee as she walked down the hill. "It's like lying to my mother."

"Why?" asked Alex. "You have no relation to her."

"Let's just focus on getting this working," said Elly, flexing her leadership muscles.

Mounira pulled out her notebook and a pencil. "What test is this?"

"Propellant," said Elly.

"Wing changes," insisted Alex.

"Wings on one of the prototypes, and then propellant," offered Mounira.

"We never have enough time, it's going to get us into trouble," said Elly, shaking her head.

"You worry too much," said Alex with a wink.

CHAPTER TWENTY-TWO
RED HOODED PLANS

Ron-Paul Silskin sat quietly, brooding. He'd hoped that Caterina would dash, not confirm, the rumors that Simon St. Malo was under investigation for treason. "The Fare's High Council isn't going to be pleased with this, not at *all*. He has supporters," he said, reaching for a pear from the ornate bowl that sat between him and Caterina.

They were sitting in a large gazebo high up above the royal gardens. Caterina often sat there when she needed to think. She enjoyed the panoramic floral beauty. It also kept everyone at such a distance as to keep civil conversations private.

"I'm less concerned with the council," replied Caterina, taking a bite out of a pear. "I'm not saying he did anything criminal, however as Regent I need to send a message that *no one* is above the law. I was well within my right to order him beheaded. Instead, he's just being kept in the guest house. One thing is clear to me, he's been up to something."

Silskin eyed her suspiciously. The sudden silence of the council and Simon being under lock and key made him nervous. He decided it best to press her on another front all together, at least to buy himself some time to think. "What about DeBoeuf? Weren't you supposed to double-cross her after freeing her as payment?"

Caterina dumped the core of her pear on a plate with a clang. She glared at Silskin. "Whose responsibility was it to ensure that all of the inventors were taken alive from Pieman's palace? And whose responsibility was it to also ensure that the morning after DeBoeuf was free, she was to be retaken?"

Silskin thought of the bungled affair, and how they'd lost nearly half of the inventors. He put his hands up. "I'm just saying I don't understand why we even had to let DeBoeuf out of her room."

Rolling her eyes, Caterina repeated herself as she had many times before, "Because that woman has many sympathizers. Had she not been allowed to be free long enough to make contact with the fringe parts of her spy network, they would have known we double-crossed her. Now, if she'd been recaptured the next day, there were any number of ways we could have handled it. But instead *you* lost her. A fact I have *not* shared with the council."

"And I'm grateful," replied Silskin, uncomfortably. He

squinted as the late afternoon sun peeked under the gazebo's roof. "All this has to do with your plan to execute Marcus, doesn't it?"

"Ah, there's the Ron-Paul who earned his place at my side," said Caterina, taking an apple from the bowl. "Once we have an agreement from the dignitaries of the four regions to strip Marcus of his Head of Country title, we can behead him. It should be easy, what with the things he's done over the years, plus *his* recent airship attacks." She stared intensely at the sweating Silskin. "Is there any question that those attacks of ours were attributed to the Piemans?"

"Not that I've heard, your highness," replied Silskin. "But what of Kar'm? Won't this be another Bodear?"

"The world knew there was a village in Bodear, so there were people to mourn it. Kar'm is a place of ruins, nothing is there as far as the world is concerned. This is purely for us. We will show our enemies we know their secrets, and that nothing is sacred."

Silskin glanced at the gardens and attendants. He was even more certain than before that Caterina's spies were watching his every move. He needed to talk with the council to make sure they were okay with her plans. She was venturing through a room full of powder keg kingdoms with a torch.

"Destiny is about taking," said Caterina, taking a bite of her apple. She wondered what would have happened if her father had married off her eldest sister instead of her, as he was supposed to. The very thought of the man curdled her blood.

"Oh, you're home," said a surprised seventeen-year-old Caterina to her father. She'd been surprised to see his study door open and had peeked inside.

Gaston Maurice turned from the window, and stared at his daughter. "Come in, Caterina. We need to have a conversation." He forced a fleeting smile.

She hesitated. He'd been strange lately. Even the way he'd ask her to come in seemed laced in something worrisome. For most of the past year, he'd been away more than he'd been home, leaving her to the torturous mercies of her two older sisters. Even when he'd been home, she'd been eclipsed from his attention by their constant wants. He was always tired and annoyed by the time she got to him.

She crept into the tomb-like office and pulled her well-worn shawl around her tightly. The wall-candles flickered. She followed her father's gaze to the frost lined window, and at the moon in the clear winter sky. The fireplace was dormant, the wood having run out earlier in the day. Like many things, while they had the means to buy more, her father had no interest in doing so.

He gestured absent-mindedly to the threadbare, low-backed chair opposite him.

Caterina shuffled her bare feet and placed herself

gingerly in the uncomfortable seat. She loathed being in that room. Nothing good had ever happened there. Sitting in that chair years before, she'd been told of her little brother's drowning death, and before that, their mother's death from fever.

With a mutter and grumble, Gaston pulled his gaze away from the moon and looked at his youngest daughter. He was in his late fifties and had a bloated belly that didn't sit well on the otherwise thin man. His crown of thick white hair was longer than it should've been for a man of his station. His beady eyes were as cold as the winter outside.

Groaning, he got up and closed the door. He wandered over to the bookcase and searched for a book. Finding it, he pulled it and returned to his chair, laying the book on his lap. He stared at his daughter, his fingers playing with his lips.

"Papa?" asked Caterina, the tension getting to her.

"Do you know what I've been doing these past several months, Caterina?"

She shook her head. "I just know it's important."

"It is." He leaned forward and scratched his grey stubble. He handed the book to her.

Its familiar feel told her she didn't even need to look at the title. The few threads that held the book together were a reminder of how much they'd been made to study it. "The Ways of Wisdom by John Fare. What does this have to do with me being here?"

"What is the book?" he asked.

"It's a treatise from the dawn of the Era of Innovation."

Gaston stroked the side of his head. It was late, and he would have preferred to have the conversation in the morning, but there wouldn't be time. "From those words came a philosophy, and then a special society; the Fare. The Fare was focused on making the world right—ending the constant wars and the social genocide that always picked some foolish trait, be it blue eyes or birthmarks on the right arm or some such nonsense, as a reason to kill people. That philosophy understood that you had to have masters behind the royal rulers, keeping them in check and giving them something real to fear. I know you know all of this, you've always been good at study," he said, paying a rare complement. "Tell me, what are people's souls made of?"

Without a second thought, she answered, knowing exactly on what page the idea was first introduced in the book. "Gold, silver, copper and wood. Each denoting the person's intended station and purpose in life."

Gaston smiled. "Now, tell me, what happens if you give the duties of a gold to a wood?" he asked, chewing on a finger.

Caterina didn't blink at the trivial questions. "They will fail horribly. Even the strongest of woods cannot serve as long as a gold, and they will bring infections to those around them. The infections are madness, corruption, pain and hunger."

He smiled again. "Unlike your sisters, you know this, you know it as I'd always intended. They are many things, your sisters, but clever is not one of them. That's what makes you precious, Caterina, that's why I don't need to worry about you.

"Now, what if I told you there was a man out there, a powerful man, who was undoing everything the Fare has tried to do? A man who has taken most of the Fare and replaced its soul with something completely the opposite."

"That… would be a danger to civilization," replied Caterina, worried. "The world needs the Fare, doesn't it? That's what you've always taught us."

"Indeed, it does," he replied, leaning forward and patting her knee. "The good news is that the world will not end tonight. But tomorrow is a different matter. I'm glad you feel as I do."

"Years ago, when the Fare was at its weakest, a charismatic and brilliant man came along, by the name of Marcus Pieman. He took the reins of power and gave the Fare a new sense of purpose. But that purpose, over time, was revealed to be less and less what the Fare had always stood for. For a while, none said a word. The day came, as some had expected, that he ignored the Council of the

Fare altogether. He wielded so much power that even they now feared him. And so it was for many years, with only some measures of protest here and there. Each time the Pieman would crush them, or else find a way to bring them to his side."

"As his sons have come into their own in recent years, those protests have become a bit of a rebellion. Now it isn't one Pieman we face, but three. There's a rumor that he's even grooming his granddaughter to stand as a fourth pillar of their empire."

Caterina's eyes told Gaston everything.

"I'd started traveling, in search of support to fight him, but instead it's become something of a different mission. I've learned that Marcus Pieman has no desire to keep our squabbles going, it drains his resources and it consumes all of ours. An offer has been made that might allow us to work together." He drummed his fingers on the arm of his chair.

"What does this have to do with me?" asked Caterina timidly.

He smiled at her, like the spider does the fly. "You said we cannot let this happen, and you're right. That is why you will marry Lennart Pieman, the younger of the two brothers. I believe—"

"What? You can't!"

Gaston slapped her. "Know your place," he barked. As she cried, he continued. "Sometimes who you were has to die so you can become who you need to be. I've certainly learned that many times, and now it's time you should. The Piemans are sending a coach for you in the morning." He stood up, his deed done. "I expect you to have some sense about this and know that it is your duty. You've been given the opportunity at a great destiny. Take it."

As her father left, she curled up in the chair and fell asleep, sobbing. A knock at the door awakened her, it was her two older sisters.

"I hear congratulations are in order," said Katherine, the eldest.

"Yes, to us. We're finally rid of you," replied Kamille, laughing.

"And all it took was us forgetting that stupid book, right Kamille?"

"There's a book? Gosh, I hadn't noticed there was a book. Gee, all those Saturdays and Sundays, for fifteen years, and you'd think I'd remember something about it, Kath."

"What?" said Caterina sitting up. "Wait, isn't the eldest daughter supposed to marry first?"

The sisters smiled. "Good luck. And enjoy being the new eldest, *Catherine*," they said laughing as they left.

Caterina took another bite of her apple. She'd been staring at the garden in silence, lost in thought. She could feel the disease within Silskin radiating. "Still worried about Kar'm, or simply enjoying the view?"

"Just enjoying the view," said Silskin, offering a flinching smile.

"So, tell me, what about Richelle Pieman?"she asked. "You told me she was dead."

"She… is."

"Simon seemed absolutely certain that the hand writing was hers." She sat up in her chair. "I'm *concerned*, Ron-Paul. I'm concerned that you aren't upholding your end of our bargain, that you're playing games behind my back or feeding me information you want me to hear, without it being true or verified."

Silskin turned away and wiped the beads of sweat from his forehead carefully. "Nothing of the sort."

Caterina glared at him. She watched as his shoulders melted and his gaze lowered. She hated it when he cowered. "Fine. You spoke with Marcus Pieman recently, how did he seem?"

Silskin squirmed, trying to find the right words. "He was distraught. A… a ghost of a man. His world has crumbled, and his secret game with Nikolas Klaus yielded nothing. And what is worse, the man has been reduced to a yammering idiot. Klaus, not Pieman. You've broken him."

Caterina had resisted the urge to strike Marcus for so long, she'd found herself wondering if she would ever do it. Was it out of fear that she waited, or her desire to grow her forces and allies before doing so? She'd found herself dropping hints, the most audacious of which was having Pieman's presidential gardens reshaped into the symbol of the Fare. She knew her impatience was leaking into her actions, and finally decided to act. But with Pieman's world smashed, she felt no different inside. She hoped that, with his death, she'd find the peace that had eluded her at her father's death.

"There is still the matter of Abeland," she said, looking for holes in their plans. "His little act of sabotage, casting Simon in a bad light, means we cannot let our guard down."

"Agreed," said Silskin.

"Excuse me, your highness," said a military man from the foot of the steps with a protesting attendant. "May I approach you and Lord Silskin? I have urgent news."

The white clothed attendant beside him gazed up nervously at the shaded gazebo, fearing a possible punishment for allowing the breach of protocol.

"Approach, Captain."

"Sorry to disturb you, but I was given this message to hand you, personally," he said handing her an envelope.

"The regent doesn't have time to read everything. What is it?" asked Silskin, impatient and nervous he wouldn't be told.

The captain waited for Caterina's approval before speaking. "The four royal dignitaries held a secret meeting with Marcus Pieman two nights ago. I was given that letter, which I was told but have not seen, is signed by all four of them. It is, as they said, the decision of the Southern, Eastern, Lower and Independent Kingdoms speaking with one voice."

"What?!" said Caterina, ripping open the seal on the letter.

Silskin wiped his face nervously. "You don't have the look of a man giving us the news we expected."

The captain stood silent, allowing the regent to finish reading the letter.

She turned a burning glare on Silskin. "And you said he was broken! *Broken!* If he was so *broken*, then how did he convince them to give him a Trial by Royals? How?!"

"He was!" protested Silskin.

She threw the letter in his face.

Silskin read it, going ever more white. "They've... they've moved him to Relna, in Belnia. He's out of our jurisdiction, your Highness. But they were supposed to strip him of his title, weren't they? There hasn't been one of these in... in centuries. Do they even have the right to request such a thing?"

"They do," replied Caterina, her voice laced with distilled anger. She glanced at the captain who was standing, a bead of sweat hanging on his nose.

She stood up, seized his pistol and shot him, kicking his dead body down the stairs. She stared at Silskin's panicked face. "Need I clean up all of your messes? I will not have my victory stolen from me, not when I am so close."

CHAPTER TWENTY-THREE

THE UNEXPECTED

As Christina marched through the corridors with Angelina, she noted the looks of those she passed change from frustration to fear to bewilderment. "What's going on? What's so important that you need me?"

"You wouldn't believe me if I told you," said Angelina, in her quick and dry manner.

With a nod, the portcullis opened, followed by the thick, wooden gate beyond it.

Christina wondered who the shadowed lone figure standing beside a horse was. He was wearing a long dark coat, and held his hands together in front of him. When the sun bounced off his monocle, she immediately knew. She turned to Angelina.

"I said you wouldn't believe me," said Angelina. Taking up her position and allowing Christina to approach Abeland by herself, she made eye contact with the hidden marksmen to ensure everyone was at the ready.

Christina scratched the side of her face as she

approached Abeland. "Did we get put on a map, because you aren't supposed to know about this place."

Abeland gave one of his most charismatic smiles. He felt like his old self, dressed in his classic clothes, his lungs working properly, and taking a risk to get something he wanted. "Hi, Christina. It's been a while." He glanced around and lowered his voice, bringing her in closer. He wanted to ensure no one could hear what he was about to say. "There are a lot of things that I'm not supposed to know. But this," he said, gesturing, "I've known about this place for quite a while. Actually, we put it on *our* map, though only my father, Richelle and I knew where it really was."

Something clicked in Christina's brain. "Bodear. You marked that it was in Bodear. That's why it was bombed, wasn't it?"

Abeland nodded.

"So, you have a mole," said Christina. "That's surprising."

"Sometimes the people you know the longest are the people you can trust the least," replied Abeland, with a less convincing smile.

"You look thin," remarked Christina.

"I chose a bad vacation destination."

"Tangears again?"

"Prison."

Christina couldn't help laughing. "Well, that *is* a bad

choice."

Abeland smiled warmly. "I left once I realized that the room service wasn't simply late."

Putting up a hand, Christina said, "Stop the charm offensive. Why are you here?"

He took a step forward, glancing about at the marksmen that stood out to him like trees on a grassy plain. "I'm not the only one with a problem in my organization. The difference is, I know mine, and he's no longer a problem."

She stared at the ground. She knew Abeland well enough to know that he wanted something in exchange. Studying his face, she could see that he wasn't likely lying. As tricky as he was, he was still very much the young man she'd met, and trusted, long ago. "Are you sure?"

Abeland reached into one of his saddle bags and pulled out a metal canister. "Do you know what this is?"

"No," she replied.

"Really? Huh. It's used in a Neumatic Tube. It took us decades, but we built rivers of them all over. They allow us to send messages quickly. Brilliant design," he said, unscrewing the lid and taking a few sheets of paper out. "Unfortunately, Caterina Maurice and her Fare have been using it, too. Well, not completely unfortunately. I wouldn't have this to offer you if they hadn't." He handed the papers over.

She studied his face. "The only Caterina Maurice I know of is—"

"It's her," quipped Abeland.

"But that's impossible."

"Yes, well, we Piemans are terribly hard to kill. Apparently even just marrying into the family can bestow that ability. Turns out her sons are alive, as well."

Christina saw the look in his eye. "So, Caterina is the Lady in Red?"

Abeland nodded.

"It's not like you to give something without a price," said Christina, uneasy.

Ignoring her statement, he continued, "I don't know how many messages your mole sent, but this one was sent four days ago. It took me longer to get here than I had hoped, but I didn't trust anyone else to come, and Richelle's busy."

"I thought Richelle was dead."

Abeland smiled wryly.

"Piemans *are* terribly hard to kill," said Christina shaking her head.

"You'll see in those papers that the mole knows about the MCM engine, and helped sabotage your rocket pack experiment. They've been leading a small group of fellow traitors in tearing your organization apart."

Christina let out a heavy sigh. "We haven't found any evidence of that. I'd hoped it wasn't just us crumbling."

"You're a good person, Christina. You always have been. Now, those papers don't have the name of the traitor, just proof that they exist."

"What good is that to me?"

"It'll make it easier for you to understand why I want what I want, in exchange for the name of the traitor." Abeland leaned in. "I propose a trade. The name of your traitor for an hour with the incomplete MCM engine. You can even have someone supervise, I don't care. I just want to see it."

Christina glanced back at Angelina, who would likely go ballistic over any deal. Then again… "That's the deal?"

"That's the deal. My father took a gamble on Klaus, sending him to Minette, hoping that he'd create a successor to the MCM, but he never did."

A smile crept against Christina's lips. She thought of the rocket-cart that they'd found, and pondered for a moment why Nikolas would have also invented the slow moving, horseless cart. She figured he must have known someone was spying on him. Glancing around at the landscape, she said, "You have a deal."

Before she even needed to ask, Abeland took another piece of paper out of his pocket. "Once you have me set up in the room, I'll give you the name of the lead traitor."

Christina opened the door and stared uncomfortably at the giddy Abeland. Though flanked by two of her best, appropriately armed guards, Abeland looked like a little boy about to have cake. She could just hear Angelina's arguments against doing this replay in her head. It had been a long walk to the lab, and it hadn't helped that she'd been accosted by several people along the way. Apparently, things were boiling over from the meeting she'd been pulled out of.

Studying Abeland's face, she thought back to the teenage boy she'd met long ago. Her father once again a prisoner, she'd been invited to stay in the Pieman's home, which was extremely awkward. One morning, she and her father would be gone, and then months later they would return, against their will. She'd only recently learned that Marcus had traded, several times, to have them handed over after they'd been captured as abominators in other jurisdictions. The relationship was very complex, to say the least.

"The room is ready. You can be here until sundown, and then you never return. If you're late, they'll kill you," she said, smirking.

"Oh trust me, this place is nice, and everything, but I have somewhere to be. I particularly like the antique dust and mold, it's a nice touch," said Abeland, gazing about. He handed Christina the paper, but as she grabbed hold of it, he held fast. "I request that you let me enter the room first, and suggest you consider reading this where you have less people about."

She nodded, and he let go.

"Gentlemen, let's us go mine the past so that the future can be created, shall we?"

"Just get in there," said the first guard.

Abeland stepped into the warmly lit room. "Well, no expense was spared, was it? I love what you've done with the place." Apart from the lantern in each corner of the ten by ten room, there was only a stool and a beaten, worn table. On it was a piece of history; an open mercury-copper-magnetic engine. He didn't even notice anything else. "Marvelous."

"You talk a lot," said the second guard.

"Well, Number Two—do you mind if I call you that? I'm sure you have a name, but here's a secret; I'm truly not interested in it. If you don't care for my antics, you're welcome to leave." He stared at the first guard. "You need a name too. I will call you Three."

"But there's two of us," replied guard number two.

"Not my problem, now is it? Fine, I'll call you One, as I fear you might lose your precious little minds otherwise," said Abeland, feasting his eyes on the engine. "Now, I have some analysis to tend to." He took off his gloves and emptied his coat pockets of some folded sheets of paper, a notebook and a pencil. Taking off the coat and folding it neatly, he looked about, a bit annoyed. "Um, may I have a chair for my coat?"

"Put it on the table, smart guy," said Number One, pointing. He was older than the second guard by at least ten years.

After sweeping the dust away with his hand and glaring at the men, he put his coat down with an annoyed huff. He rolled up his sleeves, put his pocket-watch on the table and turned a dial on his monocle. Finally ready, he started examining the engine like a spider does its tangled prey.

For several minutes he jotted down notes, carefully moved pieces and pulled out fine tools from the spine of notebook until he reached out for something that wasn't there. He stood up and looked about. "Um, where's the tea?"

"There isn't any," said Number One.

Abeland shook his head in disbelief. "No tea? Are we in the middle of a barbarian wasteland? There *must* be tea. Would you be so kind as to fetch some? There's no reason to be anything but civil. It's not like I'm asking for the King's-Horse."

Number One nodded, and then said, "You better start shutting up." He leaned on the hilt of his short-sword.

Abeland laughed. "Please. By the time you'd have that out, you'd be dead—twice. Along with your friend, here."

"Who *is* this guy?" asked Number Two.

"Nobody," replied the first guard.

Abeland laughed again. "Really? Is that why there are beads of sweat running down the side of your face?"

"It's hot," he retorted.

Number Two glanced at both of them, nervously.

"What One isn't telling you, Two, is that he knows who I am. You know the guy with the glowing monocle who goes would go to the courts of kings and queens to get them to surrender their country, or forcefully takes it?"

"I've heard those stories, but they aren't true," replied the second guard.

Abeland clicked the wheel on his monocle, making it glow. "Why don't you check with One?"

Number Two looked at his superior, who was staring at the floor. He confirmed everything with a nod and a look.

"Seriously? *That's* the guy? Yig! Why didn't we just shoot him when he got here?" asked Number Two.

"And how do you think *that* would have worked out?" asked the first.

"It's a small room," said Abeland, gesturing about. "Now, before I lose my temper and... I don't know, maybe do something that befits my reputation, would you *please* be civilized and get me a cup of tea?"

"Why are we letting him see that thing?" asked Number Two.

"Because I'm trying to save the world," replied Abeland.

"And why would you do that?"

Abeland chuckled. "Because it's Tuesday, and that's a very Tuesday thing to do."

Guard number one grumbled, and then said, "Just get him the tea."

Abeland leaned against the table. "This is what will happen if you go with that nervous twitching in your stomach, Two. You'll first go for your pistol, then change your mind to your short sword because it's close quarters and you're worried having only one shot, you might miss. By that time, your friend will be dead, and I'll have a pistol to your temple. I'll likely say something witty, confusing you for a moment, and then I'll say *why couldn't you have just gone out and gotten me a cup of tea?*"

One nudged Two, who quickly left the room.

Abeland turned back to the table, focusing on it. "Is everyone in place, Reginald?"

"They are," replied guard number one. "And to your hint about the King's-Horse, you'll take a walk over in a bit to make sure that you're all clear."

"Excellent," replied Abeland, glancing at his pocket-watch. "Hmm." He sifted through the some folded messages. "According to the traitor's notes I kept, we only have a few hours before things will get decidedly noisy here. Until then, make sure I'm not disturbed, other than for tea. Understood?"

"Yes, sir. I'll have us stand outside, with the door closed."

Abeland paused, thinking of Christina and what was about to happen. "One change of plan, actually. I need you, personally, to take care of someone when the time comes."

"What does it say?" asked Angelina for the tenth time as Christina stormed away from the lab, the paper she got from Abeland crumpled angrily in her hand. Angelina grabbed her by the shoulder. "Talk to me, Chris."

Christina's eyes were filled with fury. "Canny's brother! He's the mole!" she yelled.

Angelina thought. "I don't get it. Just calm down."

Christina shook with anger. "Canny hadn't seen his big brother since he was little, and the guy showed up six months ago, and immediately things started falling apart. I knew we shouldn't have allowed him into the meetings. I *knew* we shouldn't have skipped all our precautions to make sure we didn't have someone who could infect us. I knew it! I knew it! *I knew it!*" Her eyes burned into Angelina's as she thrust the paper into Angelina's chest. She then marched off for the meeting room, her streaming pistol now firmly in hand.

Scanning the paper quickly, Angelina suddenly understood. "Yig, I should have seen this. *All* of this."

Christina flipped up the dark wood barrel cover of her pistol, revealing a tightly wound coil. She put some pebbles in its chamber from one of her pouches and slapped it closed. "Where is he?"

CHAPTER TWENTY-FOUR

SIGNALING THE END

Christina marched down the hallway, muttering. Angelina had rushed ahead and left her to deal with everyone who insisted on sharing a piece of their mind.

Angelina stood at the doorway, blocking her path. "You can't go in there."

She was about to push Angelina out of the way and then stopped. "Why's it so quiet? And what... what's that smell?"

"You can't go in there," repeated Angelina, tears in her eyes.

For a minute, they wrestled back and forth. Though Angelina was several inches shorter than Christina, she kept her leader at bay.

"Get out of my way," commanded Christina.

"You need to calm down and listen," insisted Angelina.

Christina didn't have the energy to get angry. She

noticed that what she thought was dirt on Angelina's face and clothes *wasn't* dirt. "Is that—?"

Angelina's lip quivered. "There was an explosion. Canny's brother… he…"

"He *what*?" asked Christina, her voice raising. "Tell me!"

"He set off a bomb. I'm told Canny noticed, and Remi —"

"No," whispered Christina.

Angelina tried to continue, and then lost her grip.

"Remi!" said Christina, shoving Angelina aside and bursting into the gory room.

A red haired woman, wiping her tears, stepped away from Canny's body. "Christina, you—"

Christina took in the scene and started shaking. She wanted to scream but lacked the voice. She inched over to Remi's body.

Angelina steadied herself and said, "They jumped on him. We didn't know until I rushed in. He saw the look in my eyes, and then… I was knocked back. I couldn't save them."

Mattias was in the corner, staring at the scene. "How did this happen? One minute we were laughing, and then Canny moved, and then… *How*?"

"Come on, Matt," said the red haired woman. "Come on."

Angelina gestured for the other people to get out.

"Somehow, no one got seriously injured who wasn't killed," said Angelina. "Sonya, Remi, Canny, Frederick... somehow, they saved the others."

Christina was kneeling, sobbing. "This is all my fault."

"No, it's not," said Angelina, wiping her nose on her sleeve.

A flash of yellow appeared at the door, catching both of their eyes.

"Get her out of here... please," said Christina.

"What happened?" asked Mounira, horrified.

Angelina walked over, spun Mounira around, and marched her off.

Christina's sat there, staring at Remi's broken body. She wanted to touch his face, to say goodbye, but it would make everything real, and she couldn't have that.

"What happened? Is Christina okay?" asked Mounira. Angelina was silent as she forcefully marched her away.

"Stop!" said Mounira, awakening her mechanical arm and grabbing Angelina.

Angelina snapped out of her daze and shook off the arm. "No, she's not okay! We just lost some good people. No, great people. There was a spy from the Fare here. He blew himself up. He's the main one behind everything that's been going on."

"Were you there?" asked Mounira, her eyes wide and

worried. She slowly put her mechanical arm away.

Angelina nodded, staring at the stone floor. "I don't know how I knew, but I knew something bad was about to happen. I can't believe it." She gazed at Mounira. "You should go… play. Be a kid, for all of us."

Mounira kicked Angelina in the shins.

"What the yig?" scolded Angelina.

"We took on soldiers, Richelle Pieman and countless others, and you think I'm just a kid?"

Angelina glared at her. "Let's be real. You need to just get out of the way."

Taking a step back, Mounira glared at the taller woman. "This is just the beginning, and when things happen, you're going to need us."

"This was it," said Angelina. "They've just kicked us in our soul."

"You don't understand," said Mounira, leaving. "The people who did this, they aren't interested in kicking it. They're interested in crushing it."

———

"Where are you guys?" yelled Mounira, running down the stairs. "Guys?"

Tee and Elly looked at each other across the workbench. "That's not the happy go lucky Mounira voice," said Elly.

"No," agreed Tee. "We're here!"

Mounira popped through the doorway. "There was a

spy, he killed a bunch of people upstairs with a bomb. Christina's sobbing."

Tee and Elly stood up, instinctively grabbing their new yellow hoods from the wall hooks.

"That was the rumble we heard," said Tee, thinking.

"This isn't good," said Elly. "Should we find Alex?"

Tee put her grapple-armband on. "Help me with the backpack for the rope."

"What are you doing?" asked Mounira.

"You're going to say that you have a funny feeling, right?" asked Tee. "I can see it in your eyes."

Mounira looked at Elly and then Tee. "Yes."

"I'm starting to love and hate that feeling of yours," said Elly, putting Tee's cloak over her backpack. "Now we have two humped-back Yellow Hoods. I feel like I'm being left out."

"So how can we help Angelina and the others?" asked Tee.

"She doesn't want our help," answered Mounira.

Tee sighed. "Without Christina, no one's going to listen to us, are they?"

"No," said Alex from the doorway. "I just heard. Remi, Canny... unbelievable. I figured you'd be down here. What do we need to do?"

Tee turned to Mounira. "How bad's that feeling in your stomach?"

"Bad," she replied.

"Mine, too," said Tee. "Okay, see if you can get to Christina. We're going to need her help if you're right. Elly?"

"I'll go to the forest, get our stuff ready in case we need it. We're not really ready, but it might give us some options."

Tee nodded, and looked at Alex. "Go with Mounira. Then come and meet us in the forest."

Suddenly there was a loud rumble, and dust fell from the ceiling.

After the second violent rumble, Abeland glanced around, his concentration finally broken. "Looks like our information was a little off," he said, pulling a backpack out of his long coat and stuffing his notes in it. He looked at the second guard as he stuffed the MCM engine into his backpack as well. "Mind if I borrow this?"

"What?" said the guard.

"Well, I suppose *take* is probably a better term. I don't really intend to return it," said Abeland as the room shook. "What with this place being a pile of rubble soon, and whatnot."

As the guard went to take out his pistol, Reginald hit him in the back of the head, knocking him out.

"I was starting to wonder if you were going to let your colleague shoot me first," said Abeland, coughing from the dust in the air. "Seems the Fare's a little impatient to get things started today. Punctuality is a lost art, I tell you." He smiled at Reginald. "Now, tell me the way."

"Are you sure you want to go after the King's-Horse? It's guarded."

"You've got a job to do, and I'll be fine," answered Abeland, taking off down the corridor.

CHAPTER TWENTY-FIVE

ON TRACK

As the rail-raft slowed down, Bakon and Egelina-Marie released their iron grips on their chairs. The experience of riding up and down the hills of the Belnian landscape had been much akin to being on a ship in a mild storm, for hours.

Bakon rubbed his hands and took a deep breath. He was about to remove the ropes holding him in place when he noticed no one else had moved yet.

"Wait for it," said the soldier beside him.

Then with a massive jerk, the rail-raft came to a stop. Several of the soldiers at the long levers stumbled about.

"Dangerous job," mused Bakon.

"You should see when they have new guys, sometimes they fall clean off these things," added the soldier, untying himself.

Bakon turned to Egelina-Marie, who immediately burst into laughter.

"What?" asked Bakon.

She glanced at his hair, holding the laughter in.

"Never mind," she said, biting her lip.

"You're a bad liar."

Eg burst into laughter again.

They were quickly escorted off the rail-raft and asked to stand a dozen yards away. They watched as the soldiers and captains moved about furiously, ants attacking fallen food. A few oddly dressed people scurried about yelling wildly, Conventioneers responsible for making sure the Skyfallers were ready for operation.

As the first Skyfaller started to inflate, Egelina-Marie turned to Bakon, worried. "Why did your m— why do you think Caterina sent us here?"

Bakon shrugged. "I don't know, maybe to get us out of the way?" He saw something in Eg's eyes. "What do you think?"

"I think if we just sit back and wait, we'll end up dead."

He nodded, quickly scanning the area, looking for something in particular. "There, come on." He jogged over and grabbed one of the ropes for the second Skyfaller as it started to lift into the air.

"Hey, thanks," yelled the captain as he walked past. "We're short people today, glad to have all the extra hands we can. Lots of operations going on." He then stopped and stared at Bakon. "Wait, aren't you the Maurice?"

Bakon couldn't bring himself to agree, but Egelina-

Marie did on his behalf.

The captain snapped his fingers and flagged another soldier to take Bakon's place. "You shouldn't be doing that. Grab the rope ladder, you're flying with me."

Egelina-Marie marveled at the behemoth. "I'm not sure this is a good idea," she whispered to Bakon.

He patted her on the shoulder. "I don't think we *do* good ideas."

"Over there!" yelled Richy to Amami. "I saw something shining in the sunlight!"

Amami brought them alongside it and slowed the King's-Horse down. "Finally. I am thankful that this endeavor is not fruitless."

They'd been hunting for rails for three days, and decided to ignore Eleanor's request for them to stay and wait for her return. Shortly after she'd headed off to meet with Sam and their potential allies, Amami and Richy had grabbed their hoods and left.

Richy smiled. "You have a funny way of speaking Frelish sometimes. But I like it."

"I have been told some of the eight languages that I speak sound that way. Informality comes with practice," she replied.

"Eight? I'll shut up now," said Richy. He dismounted and looked in both directions down the rails. "Someone went through a lot of trouble to put these here. I can see where the trees were ripped out. See the new growth? It's probably been three or four years."

Amami was impressed. "How do you know that?"

"You learn a lot when you live in the mountains, surrounded by forests," he replied. "We had a great mentor, too. He died."

"I am sorry." Bending down, she put her hands on a rail.

"What are you doing?"

"If they are moving anything on these, the way Madame DeBoeuf said, then the metal will tell us if it is nearby. It will vibrate, sending a feeling through it, even if we can't hear it." She smiled at him. "I've learned different things."

Richy put his own hands on the other rail. "Is that something?"

She nodded.

"Is something going away or coming?" asked Richy.

"It is fading. It came by here recently, and it is big," said Amami pensively. "Which direction do you think it is going?"

Glancing about, Richy pointed westward.

"I think so, too."

They jumped back on the King's-Horse, and within minutes found a train of rail-carts and rail-rafts coming to a stop. Hidden among the trees, they carefully watched as people poured out and started working away.

"Do we go back and tell Madame DeBoeuf what we found?" asked Richy after a while.

Amami shook her head. "Not yet. We don't know anything."

"We know that there's a bunch of soldiers, and some Red Hoods and... wait, is that thing inflating? That's a giant air balloon."

"No, it's *two* giant air balloons," said Amami.

They were captivated as the Skyfaller started to take shape and rise up. Soldiers hung on to ropes every few feet, controlling its ascent and allowing bombs to be loaded on.

"We need to go," said Richy. "This has to be that big thing."

Amami's face went red. "We are going to destroy those. They are abominations. The Fare cannot be allowed to have them."

"Okay, what do we do?" asked Richy, grabbing a shock-stick and charging it.

They ran for the King's-Horse. "We're going to grab a rope and climb into one of them. We'll figure the rest out when we are inside the ship."

Richy smiled. "We definitely are related."

They bolted past the first set of soldiers before anyone knew what was happening. As Amami skidded the King's-Horse to a stop they sprang off, knocking aside soldiers holding on to ropes for the second Skyfaller.

Shots started to fire as the airship lifted, but were quickly called off.

Two people looked down on them from the Skyfaller.

Amami secured her grip and took out a thin, strange looking tube.

"Watch out!" yelled Richy as a soldier fell right past them. "How did that happen?"

They both gazed up as another soldier shot passed them.

"What the heck is going on up there?" asked Richy.

CHAPTER TWENTY-SIX
KAR'M'IC
TRAPPINGS

"Wait up!" Alex yelled as Mounira swam through the stream of people. All of a sudden, the flash of yellow that he'd been following disappeared. "Mounira? Where did you go?"

Mounira slammed into an old table. She noticed the window over head, then turned to see the man that had grabbed her. "Anciano Stein?"

The tall bald man's glasses seem to take up half his face. He locked the door to the small room and straightened up. "Sorry, Mounira, but I do so hate that title. My name is Doctor Francis Stein, but you can call me Doctor Stein, for short," he said, his hands clasped together. "With all the chaos, it should be obvious no one will hear you. And if we can, I'd like to make this quick and professional. Please give me that arm of yours."

With a jerk of her head, Mounira brought her mechanical arm to life. "You're one of them?"

"Them?" wondered the doctor, pulling a knife from underneath his jacket. "Whomever you mean, no. I know opportunity when it arises. I need the arm for my research. I don't want to have to kill you, but I will. The difference is simply the amount that you'll scream before giving me the arm."

Mounira clenched her jaw. "Who said I was going to be the one screaming?" She stepped forward and hyper-extended the arm, grabbing the doctor and throwing him against a wall.

The stunned doctor got back to his feet. "Impressive, I didn't realize it had that capability. But this only postpones the inevitable." He lunged at her with his knife.

Mounira blocked his arm and tried to sweep his legs, but slipped.

"Sorry, truly," he said pouncing.

She rolled out of the way, and then, with her feet firmly planted, hit him square in the jaw with her mechanical fist. Doctor Stein fell on her, knocking her back into the chunky wooden table, before he hit the ground, unconscious.

"Me, too," she said, smiling. "Hey, I think that sounded like Elly. I'm getting good at this Frelish."

The building rumbled again, raining a grey haze of dust down. Coughing, Mounira wiped her face and glanced up. A wooden beam had broken and was dangling precariously above her.

As she tried to head for the door, she found her mechanical arm wouldn't move. She was pinned to the table. She tugged on it as hard as she could, but the arm was embedded into the soft wood.

After a minute of fighting with it, Mounira broke out in a cold sweat. She glanced at the unconscious Doctor Stein and then at the loose wooden beam above. "Come on!" she screamed, but the table refused to release her.

The building shook again and the wooden beam creaked even more. "Come on!" she screamed, looking around furiously. "Mama, are you there? Can you hear me?" Her hand was sweaty and shaking.

Mounira caught sight of something out the window, and watched. "What is that? An... air balloon ship?" As something fell from the airship, the beam creaked menacingly. She tugged with everything she was worth, and then she heard it. The leathery sound of freedom.

Christina sat there, staring at Remi's face. His dead eyes gazed at the far wall. His face was covered in blood, his armored chest horribly dented. His final expression was one of determination. She thought of all the arguments they'd had over the years, how it had taken a standstill of fighting skill to make them consider being friends long, long ago. Her mind kept gravitating to lost opportunities and spoiled moments.

She coughed as the stone dust from the loosening

blocks over head rained down on her. She was oblivious to the violent shaking and the screams from the corridors. She turned and looked at Canny's body, rolled over and facing away. She hated that she hadn't been able to figure out why he'd been so uncharacteristically angry. She'd been blinded by how happy he'd been at having a best friend.

Looking around the room, she saw regret after regret, failure after failure. Her body wouldn't move, other than her eyes and head. The world shook, and she slumped over on to her side, bringing her face to face with a fallen stone block. As wood rained down from the ceiling, she closed her eyes. She just wanted to sleep, to quickly slip away from everything.

Her eyes opened to two familiar faces gazing down at her. The first one was young and tanned, with bright, worried eyes. The second was a man, shaking her by the lapels of her leather coat. His eyes... she hadn't seen concern like that in them before.

"Abeland?" she muttered before passing out.

CHAPTER TWENTY-SEVEN

UP FOR THE FIGHT

"Sir, we've got company! Two of them hanging on the ropes below!" yelled one of the Skyfaller soldiers on the to the captain.

"I *said* we didn't need those ropes! No one ever listens," muttered the engineer to himself.

The soldiers started arguing with each other, and then with the captain, as to what they should do.

Egelina-Marie and Bakon glanced over the edge.

"Is that—?" asked Eg.

"It is. I don't know who the other one is, but any friend of Richy's is a friend of ours," said Bakon with a smirk. "I got a plan."

"What is it?" she asked, his smirk catching on.

"Clumsy ruffian," he replied as two soldiers came to join them at the edge, pistols out. He bumped into the first one and Eg following his lead. "Hey, careful!" And before the soldiers knew what was happening, Bakon grabbed the first by the belt and sent him over the edge. Egelina-Marie quickly did the same thing. He then took firm hold of one of the ropes as Eg blocked the captain's view of him and started hauling up its passenger.

"Captain, tell your men to be careful!" said Egelina-Marie. "We have two overboard!"

"What? How did that happen?" yelled the captain. "Look, you bunch of novices, this is *not* like a regular ship, so be careful! The Lady in Red will have our heads if we fail! We're already late in participating in the bombing!"

The engineer was cowering at the back of the ship where the secured bombs were stored. One look from Bakon was enough to tell him to sit and be quiet, which he quickly complied with.

"What's he doing?" yelled one of the soldiers, finally peeking around Eg. "He's helping them!"

From the side of the ship, a black cloaked figure sprang into the air and grabbed hold of the mast. Amami pulled out a coiled pipe and pointed it at one of the soldiers. With a high pitched sound and sudden rush of wind, he flew off the edge.

Egelina-Marie disarmed a soldier, took his pistol and shot another in the shoulder. As a fight ensued with the remaining soldiers, Bakon hauled Richy up and over.

"Great to see you," said Richy, throwing a shock-stick over Bakon's shoulder and dropping a soldier to the ground.

"Same here," replied Bakon with a huge grin. "Who's

the black hood?"

Amami landed on the last soldier, knocking him out cold. "I am his sister, Amami."

"Sister?" said Bakon and Egelina-Marie in unison.

"Yeah," replied Richy, picking up his shock-stick off the deck. "I'll fill you in when we're back on the ground. What do we do know?"

"That's what I was wondering," replied the engineer.

Amami scanned about. "This bloated flying pig, is this as fast as it goes?"

"Unless there's a strong gust of wind, yes," he replied, glancing at the captain.

"We need to get close to one of the other airships, see if we could throw some of those bombs over on them and take them out before them destroy everything. Look," said Egelina-Marie, pointing at the destruction taking place.

Amami pulled a sword off her back and pointed it at the engineer. "Make this ship go faster."

"I can't! I'm giving her everything she's got," said the engineer. He put his hands up defensively as sweat ran down his round face.

Bakon walked over and grabbed the captain's belt. "I'm sure we can figure out how to make this fly. Any motivational words for your engineer, or do you want to see if you can fly on your own?"

"Do as they ask, Mister Scott!" ordered the captain.

"You're right, Richy. I like your friends," said Amami.

Tee and Elly yanked off the camouflage tarps, revealing their two prototypes and several large wooden trunks.

"Tee, don't look back there," said Elly, turning back to their equipment.

Glancing over her shoulder, Tee steadied her sudden surge of emotion. From high on the forested hill, she could see the old ruined castle, parts of it streaming smoke. The scene instantly reminded her of her Grandpapa's place burning, and then seeing all of Mineau burning in the distance. Two of the Skyfallers were circling, dropping fiery vengeance, while another approached. "Elly, this... this is too much."

Elly snapped her fingers in Tee's face. "Hey, stop looking at the reality. If I've learned anything from you, it's that you don't let how insane the real world is get in your way. For a minute back in that lab, you were *you* again. Giving orders, thinking in a crisis. That's one of the things you're great at."

Tee stared at her best friend. Her face held so much determination, so much conviction, that it was hard to argue with. Hard, but not impossible. "Elly, I'm just going to get more people killed."

Elly punched Tee hard in the shoulder.

"Ow! What the heck, Elly?"

With a finger in Tee's face, Elly said, "You stared into the abyss to save me. You never need to fear about falling in. You didn't with me dying beside you. I know you to your core, you would have never killed that man. And with me saved, I will forever be your unbreakable rope. You can jump into that abyss, and I will always, always, pull you out."

Tee stared at her, the seconds ticking by. "What if you lose me because I do something stupid? What if I sent you into the abyss? I couldn't handle that."

Elly's eyes glanced around thinking. With a wicked smile, she stared back at Tee. "You'd be dead. You'd get over it."

Laughing, Tee nodded. "Okay."

"Really?" asked Elly.

"Yeah."

Alex ran up, out of breath. He looked about. "Where's Mounira?"

"Wasn't she with you?" asked Tee.

Bending over to catch his breath, he replied, "I lost her. Thought she came here."

Tee looked at Elly.

"That girl's going to find her way out. She's tough," said Elly. "Alex, let's get these things working. Tee, what's the plan?"

For an uncertain moment, Tee looked at them each in turn. "First, let's get the chemicals and everything set, then haul these two rocket-packs to the edge of the forest, so we don't have to dodge trees. Okay?"

Alex and Elly nodded.

"Does anyone else think this is a crazy idea that's likely going to get someone killed?" asked Alex.

"Nope," replied Tee and Elly in unison.

After getting the first of the rocket-pack ready, Tee and Alex hauled it out carefully to the edge of the forest.

"They're getting pounded," said Tee, gazing at the battlefield below.

"I hope someone arrives to help. I mean really, what can we do?" asked Alex, heading back.

Elly continued working furiously until she saw Alex. "Where's Tee?"

He glanced over his shoulder. "She should be right behind me."

"Oh, no," yelled Elly, bolting past him. "Tee! Wait!"

With the heavy rocket-pack strapped on, Tee put her cloak on over top. She stumbled under the weight before hitting the ignition.

"Tee, wait! The wings, they aren't—" screamed Alex as Tee shot into the sky.

Elly and Alex watched, aghast, as Tee spiraled in the air, and then sighed in momentary relief as she moved straight for one of the Skyfallers. Suddenly, the rocket pack broke apart.

"The wings mechanism—" gasped Alex.

Elly stared in horror.

Suddenly, Tee jerked in the air and started moving towards the Skyfaller quickly, one arm leading the way.

"What the—?" said Alex, dumbfounded.

"Her armband! That's my girl! That's MY GIRL!" yelled Elly, fist pumping the air.

"Wait, the thing she made? The thing she was wearing on her arm?"

"Yeah. It's a little piece of her Grandpapa. Inspired by what saved her months ago when she needed it most," said Elly, wiping away her tears.

Alex's expression suddenly went stony. "The people on that ship, they're going to have guns."

"I need to get up there," said Elly, running back.

"Sorry Elly," said Alex, running up to her and pushing her over. He bolted out of sight.

Arriving precious seconds before Elly, Alex slipped on the rocket-pack and pulled out its wings. Slapping on some goggles, he took a deep breath and pushed the ignition button. Immediately he launched into the air.

"Alex!" yelled Elly, as she watched him make a beautiful streak straight to Tee's airship. She laughed, shaking her head. "You might just be a Benjamin, Alex."

Elly looked at the spare parts and chemicals. "I've got to help them…" she snapped her fingers and started filling her backpack.

CHAPTER TWENTY-EIGHT

To Air is Human

"What's that?" asked Bakon as a yellow-tipped white streak rocketed into the air in front of them. It spiraled and bent its arc, heading roughly in the direction of the airship they were pursuing. Suddenly, the white part separated from the yellow. "Wait, that's a person..."

"That hair, the yellow... that's Tee!" yelled Richy. "She's falling out of the sky!"

Egelina-Marie cupped her mouth with her hands. "Oh, my—"

A little black line shot out from Tee and into the side of the Skyfaller.

"Huh? She's reeling herself in? What have I missed? Tee, that's awesome!" yelled Richy, knowing she couldn't hear him.

"That girl," laughed Egelina-Marie.

Out of the corner of her eye, Amami noticed the captain slowly reaching for something. With a quick two-step, she had her blade on his chest. "I wouldn't do that, Captain. I am certain I can fly this ship of yours. Having you alive is a convenience. Do you understand?"

He nodded, nervously.

"Did I mention I like her?" asked Egelina-Marie. She searched around, finally finding a rifle in one of the long boxes that lined the edge of the deck, most of them filled with ropes and tools.

"Look, another one," said Richy, pointing at a second white streak flying through the sky. This one arced beautifully and landed on the ship that Tee was just climbing aboard. "Whatever that is, I need one."

Bakon laughed. "Okay, that's probably Elly."

"Without a yellow hood?" asked Richy.

Bakon shrugged. "Who else is crazy enough to go after Tee?"

"Good point," replied Richy.

"Eg, can you take shots yet at the soldiers over there?"

She shook her head. "I know we're around a hundred yards, but given the windows up here, and how they're moving and we're moving, I don't want to risk hitting our friends. I'll try when we hit fifty yards."

"I have a better idea," said Amami. She turned to the engineer. "Bring us up. I want us above and beside that airship."

The engineer looked at the captain and received a reluctant nod. "We're going to run out of fuel quickly if we keep doing this type of nonsense," he grumbled. He walked over and spun a set of wheels, and the airship's front balloon pulled the ship up on an angle. The captain then threw the wheel, titling the ship to one side.

"Hang on, Eg!" yelled Bakon, grabbing the edge of the ship and her hand as she started to slide away.

The captain pulled out a pistol and shot, hitting Richy, but the bullet bounced off his yellow cloak. Before he could fire again, Amami plunged her sword into him, removed it and kicked him off the ship. She stabbed the deck with her blade and took the wheel. "Riichi! Get your friends' attention. Eg, prepare those bombs. Soldier-throwing-man, get the ropes ready."

"Is that me?" asked Bakon.

"No, it's the other ruffian," replied Eg, giving him a sarcastic slap on the arm.

Something flew past them, narrowly missing the two giant air balloons.

"What was that?" yelled Amami.

Bakon looked over the edge. "Richy, your eyes are better than mine. Is that Elly?"

Richy rushed over and laughed. "Elly!" he yelled, futilely.

"I think she shot something at us," said Egelina-Marie.

Richy took off his cloak and waved it at the small figure below. A yellow cloak waved back at them. "Phew... okay, so hopefully Elly won't shoot us out of the sky now."

"That's a relief," said Bakon laughing.

Snapping his fingers, Richy turned to Eg. "Do you still have that small mirror you had back in Mineau?"

"I think so, why? Oh, I get it." Egelina-Marie reached into her small pack she'd been allowed to carry with her. "Here!" She tossed it to Richy.

Tee stood there on the hillside with the rocket-pack on her back, staring up at a Skyfaller. The destruction it was raining down was unlike anything she'd seen. Her thumbs rubbed on the leather shoulder straps as she imagined all the memories and lives being destroyed. "Those poor people," she whispered.

She glanced back at Alex who was running to Elly. In a moment Elly would realize she was missing, and would know something was wrong. They both knew the idea of flying was insane, and as much fun as the project had been, they'd silently known that common sense would prevail and they would do something else. As bombs exploded, Tee couldn't shake a particular thought. "These people need the impossible."

Holding her breath, she nervously checked she was wearing her goggles. She looked tearfully at her grapple armband, her little piece of Grandpapa she had on her, and nodded to it, as if approval had been given. With a yell, she flipped the switches along the side of the rocket-pack and shot into the air.

The rocket-pack had a mind of its own, and

reluctantly relented to Tee's attempts to steer it. Finally, with herself pointed at an airship and with ten seconds of estimated flight time left, she felt something give in one of the straps. Before she knew it, she saw the rocket-pack fly away from her as she started to tumble through the air.

Time seemed to slow as Tee's mind raced, and she fought back the images of her life flashing before her. Catching a glimpse of her armband, she thought back to how her Grandpapa had saved her life by putting the same type of mechanism in her sail-cart that had saved her life at the last minute. Doing her best to stop spinning, she pointed her arm at the airship's hull and pulled the trigger of her armband. She didn't breathe as the bolt and cable shot out and finally bit into the dense wood. Laughing, she pulled a lever and the armband started to bring her of the left side of the ship.

Tee peeked over the back edge. There were six soldiers on the main deck, a captain at the helm and an engineer leaning over the far edge. Curious, she studied the two soldiers who were also leaned over. "Don't have the stomach for it, boys?" she wondered, quickly crawling onto the deck.

With her shock-sticks charged, Tee ran past the captain, smacking him in the head to distract him as she flipped forward and shocked two soldiers. The two soldiers she'd thought were being sick had really been dropping bombs. They grabbed her by the arms and hauled her into the air.

Just then, a white streak came and crashed onto the deck. As wood splintered everywhere, Tee took advantage of the moment and got herself clear of the soldiers.

"Alex?" she said, helping him up. "What are you doing here?"

"Saving you?" he offered as he fell to one knee, stunned. He was seeing double.

"Ah, sure. Why not," she replied with a wink.

Alex swallowed hard at the sight of four soldiers with their pistols pointed at them.

"Shoot them and throw them overboard," commanded the captain. "We have a job to do!"

Suddenly ropes fell onto the deck.

"Who's that?" asked Alex, pointing.

Tee followed his gaze to another airship that was dangerously close and slightly higher in the sky. "Friends! Come on!" she said, pulling him over to one of the ropes and tying him to one. Suddenly the ship started to bank and Tee slid away.

"Tee!!" yelled Alex. "What are those?" he wondered as he saw light black balls being dropped onto the deck. "Bombs? Those are bombs! *Tee*!!!"

She held on to the mast as the ship started to veer away at a sharp angle. Alex hauled himself up to the edge of the ship and untied himself.

"What's he doing?" wondered Egelina-Marie as she

prepared to shoot another soldier.

"No way," said Richy as Alex carefully ran along the edge of the ship and jumped at the captain. "I think I just found my new best friend."

Surprising the captain, Alex threw the wheel in the other direction, making the ship go back in the opposite direction.

"Eg!" yelled Richy, pointing at the captain. "Tee's got the rope, she'll get to him if you can take out the—"

BLAM!

"If I take out the captain? Got it," replied Egelina-Marie with a smile.

Richy hugged Tee the instant she was on board, and grabbed Alex's hand. "I'm Richy, and that was amazing."

"Oh, thank you," replied Alex.

Suddenly, the third airship exploded.

"What was that?" yelled Tee.

"I think Elly hit them with one of her rockets," said Bakon.

"Rockets?" said Tee and Alex, looking at each other.

"Grab on to something!" yelled Amami as she steered their airship quickly away from the other just before it exploded.

"We're hit!" screamed the engineer, pointing at one of the balloons. "We're going to die!"

"No, we aren't!" yelled back Amami. "Everyone, grab

on to something tightly. We're going to land very soon."

Elly's mood flipped from jubilant to horrified as she shifted her attention from the airship she'd just blown to bits to the one with her friends that seemed to be dropping out of the sky too quickly. "Guys, what's going on?" she said to herself. She looked at all of her rocketing supplies that were strewn about and shook her head, taking off in the direction of the troubled Skyfaller.

As she rounded a corner of the castle, she saw dark cloaked figures come into view. Reaching into her yellow cloak, she pulled out her shock-sticks and prepared for battle. She slowed to a stop as an old woman and several of the dark grey cloaks closed ranks, boxing her in.

"Elly," said the old woman.

"Get out of my way," she replied.

"I was hoping to find you here."

"I don't know who you are, but I have to get to my friends. In case you hadn't noticed, they're falling out of the sky," said Elly pointing.

The woman glanced up and leaned on her cane. "Unless you're able to fly, there's nothing you can do for them. And I'm certain Amami has everything under control."

"Who's Amami?" asked Elly, eyeing the strangers surrounding her.

"Richy's sister," the woman replied. "These are

Moufan-Men, and I am—"

"Sorry, out of my way," said Elly, springing forward.

One of the Moufan-Men stepped forward and parried every blow Elly could throw at her. With elegance and grace, she threw Elly to the ground time and time again.

The woman gestured to Elly's opponent. "The Moufan-Men are experts in many things, and hand to hand combat is one of them. Please, you need to stop and listen. I'm not your enemy," said the woman. "You may give her back her shock-sticks."

The Moufan-Man handed Elly her sticks and helped her up before returning to stand beside her colleagues.

"Who are you? And why do you look... proud? Because your people beat me?" asked Elly, glancing up at the sky as the ship fell behind the castle ruins.

"I am Eleanor DeBoeuf, the Butcher of the Tub, and I am your grandmother," said the woman with a tearful smile.

"What?" replied Elly, taking a step backwards. "Is this a trick?"

"You are Eleanor DeBoeuf, Junior. Well, I am the senior to your junior. Come," she said, offering her hand. "Your friends are going to be okay, but let's go make sure. Though battle is won, we have much to do if we are to win the war."

CHAPTER TWENTY-NINE

JOURNEYS AHEAD

Christina felt a dampness on her face. As her eyes opened, she saw the grass of the clearing. She sat up and oriented herself, rubbing her pounding head. There were voices coming from a creek behind some huge boulders a dozen yards away. She gazed above the forest's tree line at the plumes of smoke in the sky to the south, finding herself thankful that she couldn't see the ruins of her life's work.

Forcing her weary body up, she steadied herself and ran fingers across her belt pouches, counting them as always. Half way to the creek, she saw a familiar face come around a boulder.

"I thought I heard you up," said Mounira. Her face was dirty and tired. "Can you understand me? You couldn't when you woke up earlier."

Christina nodded. "Yeah. How did I get here?" She rubbed her forehead. "Abeland?"

Mounira stared at the ground, thinking. They'd been there in the forest for hours. "I think so. I don't remember if the stranger said who he was. He heard me yelling your name and came to help me, though he was cursing a lot. He said it wasn't the plan, and grumbled about time."

With a chuckle, Christina replied, "That's him." She looked at Mounira and her surroundings. She felt emotionally detached from everything, like a ship in a harbor, able to see the shore but not connected to it.

Mounira glanced around the boulder to make sure everything was okay, and then at the distracted Christina.

"A man came by a few hours ago, after Abeland and I got you here. His name was... Randle? Regal?"

"Reginald?" asked Christina. She'd remembered assigning him personally to watch Abeland.

"That's it," said Mounira, her usual exuberance lacking.

She furrowed her brow. "What did he want?"

"He said he was sorry about the engine, and—"

Christina shook her head, "He helped Abeland steal the MCM engine..." Her cheeks flushed as she started to get angry.

"Stop, there's something more important. Your father, they saved him."

"*They* who?" asked Christina.

"Reginald had two men with him, and they brought Christophe here. He's around the corner. I've been keeping him company. He comes and goes, sometimes able to focus, but... he's worried about you. Come, he's going to wonder where I am."

Christina shook her head. "No. I can't." Her face filled with grief and sadness. "I can't go through that again. No."

"What?"

"No, I can't. We went through years like that." She looked at the confused face staring at her. "I know how you feel about family, but I feel differently. I just... I can't take him being here and then not. I was relieved when it stopped."

"But, when I told you about my arm...?" replied Mounira.

She pushed Mounira's hair back over her ears. "That was different. That was a moment of him being truly him, and maybe he'll have some moments like that again, but... it's not the same. I can't watch him fall apart again."

"But we can't leave him here," said Mounira, pointing.

The approaching figure stopped and said, "There you are. You must be Mounira. Your friends are worried about you. I am Eleanor DeBoeuf."

"Are you Elly's aunt?" Mounira immediately saw the resemblance.

A smile snuck out as Eleanor was taken aback. "Actually, I'm her grandmother. Very astute."

A tall Moufan-Man accompanied Eleanor as she

approached. "We've been looking everywhere for you both. Greetings, Mademoiselle Creangle."

"Butcher," replied Christina sharply.

"There's no reason for that. If it hadn't been for my and Sam's work at getting the Moufan-Men's help, you wouldn't be alive right now."

"Their help always comes with a price," said Christina. "What did you give them? The vault?"

"No, but it is empty, I am told," replied Eleanor. "No, *we* paid the price. A very high one, if I might add."

Feeling unwelcome, Mounira interrupted, "I'm going to find my friends. See you later."

"Bye," said Christina before turning a hostile gaze back at the Butcher.

"You've been through quite a lot today. I know what it's like to have your world fall apart," said Eleanor.

"That's how you got your name, isn't it? Butcher?" replied Christina.

"Tread carefully," replied Eleanor. "I will grant you some grace because of what happened, but it is not infinite. You should have listened to my warnings that I sent you, but your distrust of the Tub, like always, clouded your judgement. You played into their hands, and you will need to live with that."

"You have—" Christina stopped herself. "What do you want? I know you didn't come here to argue politics."

Eleanor offered a polite smile. "No, I did not. Today's been an overwhelming day. We barely got the information we needed to be able to help at all. I wish we had arrived sooner. I came with my friend, here, as the Moufan-Men want to extend a most generous offer to you."

Christina studied the Moufan-Man. He was taller than Eleanor by a few inches, and had a slack face, decorated by a thin mustache. "We would like to offer you passage to our capital city in Dery, and to take care of your father." His voice was deep and warm.

"For how long?" asked Christina. She'd dealt with a few of his kind over the years. She didn't trust them or their ways, though she had nothing other than rumor to base her judgement off of.

"Until his end," replied the Moufan-Man. "It would be an honor for us. He has saved Moufan-Men at every turn over the years, and there are stories of him getting recaptured because of it. We owe him a debt."

"And you're hoping he still has some inventions left in him," sniped Christina. She quickly gestured an apology.

"You may come and go as you want," he said.

Christina stared at Eleanor, something wasn't sitting right with her. "Why are you doing this? We aren't friends, not even close."

Eleanor leaned on her cane and stared at Christina right in the eyes. "Because, despite the pain that you have been over the years, despite our requests for help that you ignored, despite having just lost the only MCM engine and the last of the original King's-Horses, I wanted to say thanks."

"For what?"

"For getting my granddaughter safely to me," replied Eleanor.

"Oh, good, a fire," said Mounira as she came into view. The evening had come about quickly, and a surprising cold had come with it.

"Mounira!" cheered Richy, Elly, Tee and Alex as she came into view. They sprang up from the campfire and ran over. Tee, Elly and Richy took turns hugging Mounira. Alex offered his hand and Mounira shook it with a smile. Despite looking messy and tired, he still had a certain dignity about him.

"Where have you been?" asked Tee. "We were worried. The Moufan-Men kept insisting you were fine. We spent hours helping them go through the ruins, looking for any survivors."

"There weren't many," added Richy.

"I was with Christina," replied Mounira.

Elly glanced past Mounira. "I don't see her."

"The Moufan-Men are apparently going to take care of her and her father. Something like that," she replied.

"That's all great, but I want you to meet someone,"

said Richy, taking Mounira by the hand.

"Who?" she asked, glancing at everyone.

"His sister," replied Elly.

"What? You have a sister?" asked Mounira excitedly.

"She does not have her mechanical arm," pointed out Alex.

Tee nodded. "I noticed that. She doesn't seem to be bothered by it."

"She'll tell us later, when there's a lull in the conversation," said Elly. "The moment she knows everyone is listening. She's reliable that way."

Tee chuckled. "Yeah, she is. I can't imagine what it'll be like when she goes home one day."

The three of them looked at each other in silence,. There was an ominous air about Tee's remark.

"So, we flew today," said Alex. "I think we made history."

Elly nodded.

Tee punched Alex in the shoulder. "Thanks, by the way," she said, smiling. Then she went over to Mounira, Richy and Amami.

Alex stared at Elly, confused. "Can you translate?"

Elly smiled mischievously. "I could," she said, and then followed Tee.

Everyone went quiet as a group of Moufan-Men approached, surrounding an old but spritely woman.

"Hello everyone. Thank you for waiting. It has been a harrowing day for all of us, and your efforts made the difference between some survivors and none. For those that haven't met me, I am Eleanor DeBoeuf. I was also known as the Butcher of the Tub."

Tee and Elly glanced at each other. "Was?" they whispered to each other.

"Our plan is to camp here this evening before we head out. We have much work to do together, and I believe it is always best to get to know one another as quickly as we can. Come, let's be around the fire. The evening is creeping in, and I for one am tired and hungry." She turned and requested something of one of the Moufan-Men.

"If we are to talk about such things, then where are Bakon and Egelina-Marie?" asked Amami. Everyone else nodded in support.

Eleanor stared at the ground and then at each of the faces. "We have very few people left to us who aren't already around this camp fire. We have few spies or allies, little money... we need to rely on each other. You all escaped what happened in Freland, but we don't know where things stand now. Monsieur Cochon and Mademoiselle Archambault have volunteered to go home and find out. We will likely meet up with them in a few months."

Tee frowned. "Didn't my dad tell you everything you

needed to know?" she asked.

"We haven't heard from William since this all began," replied Eleanor. She stared at Tee and Elly. "Why, is there something I should know?"

Tee and Elly both wondered what was going on with her father.

Mounira picked up the cue and changed the subject. "Why did you say that you *were* known as the Butcher? Is there someone new now serving as the Butcher?"

Eleanor sighed and carefully sat down. She crossed her legs and put the cane aside. "The Moufan-Men are our only remaining allies, and they are expensive. We gave to them the last thing we had; the Tub itself."

"Isn't it just an idea?" asked Richy.

"It's more than that. There are titles, roles, revenues promised and committed. Everything that remained, and a bit more, we gave to them for their help today."

"One of the things," said a voice coming out of the bushes, "is they will see us safely to Relna." The man pulled back the hood of his dark green cloak and offered a bushy-bearded smile.

"Granddad!" said Tee, springing up and over to him.

Eleanor gestured to Sam. "Everyone, I'd like you to meet, Samuel Baker. The Baker of the Tub."

"Hello, Elly. Hi, Richy," said Sam as he hugged Tee. "It's good to see you, my dear."

"It's good to see you too, Granddad," replied Tee,

returning to her spot.

"Sam, I take it that all the preparations were made?" asked Eleanor.

He nodded. "They were. I even managed to get agreement on the final matter. They've agreed."

Tee took note of an unspoken look shared between them.

"So, what's next?" asked Mounira.

Sam warmed his hands on the fire. "We go to Relna and rescue Nikolas. Then, we take advantage of the spectacular shopping and finally we stop the world as we know it from losing its mind."

"Losing its mind as in…?" wondered Richy.

"Everyone fighting everyone," answered Alex, his tone showing the idea hit home a little hard.

Gesturing to the sky, Eleanor said, "Those airships you saw today, that's just the beginning. If we aren't successful, military madness will spread. Every country will erupt in war with its neighbor. Caterina has taken over the Piemans' dangerous game and lost control."

"We're going to stop a war?" asked Mounira, her eyes wide.

"*And* do some shopping," added Sam.

CHAPTER THIRTY

TRAINED ON THE MORALE HORIZON

As Franklin gave the command, the first ever functioning steam train started slowing down. It was two stories of metal and wood, a juggernaut of new world might. He'd been shocked out of his mind when he took the reins from Simon and discovered that the Lady had everything ready. They'd been experimenting for two years trying to get a steam engine working. And it had been him, Franklin Charles David Watt, who had stepped into the middle of what seemed like random noise and turned it into a beautiful orchestra.

With knees weak from excitement, he climbed down the train's ladder and marveled at the steady feeling of firm ground under his feet. He'd wondered why Caterina had wanted to go to what looked like the middle of nowhere, only to realize now that it was her largest military encampment. People were pouring out of tents and staring slack-jawed at his invention. He grinned with pure delight as the soldiers stood in stunned silence.

The ever-growing crowd's attention moved to Caterina as she came down the ladder after him, her red cloak bright against the dark steel of the train. She stopped halfway and pointed to Franklin on the ground. She then smiled and started clapping. The crowd followed her lead, erupting in cheers and applause.

Franklin soaked it up, his eyes watering. It felt like divine sunlight as it burned away the inner doubts and fears. Everything he'd done had led to this moment, and therefore every action had been the right one. He felt like a giant among men, or more like a giant restored after having been cursed and shrunken. He looked up at Caterina as she waved for the crowd to fall silent.

"You have all just witnessed history change. As the horse and cart were to walking, the Watt steam train is to the horse and cart. With our Skyfallers ruling the world from the sky, the train will give us command of the land. Our time is almost at hand!"

The crowd erupted in cheers and applause once again.

Caterina quickly descended and put her hand on Franklin's shoulder. "It is rare that someone of your age makes such a dent in history. I look forward to what you do next. Come, now, and join me for the meeting with my generals. It might give you some ideas. Shall we, Master Conventioneer Watt?"

Franklin blushed. "Yes. Yes, please."

As they walked toward a large tent in a sea of smaller ones, she asked, "I heard you decided your father's fate while I was away in Relna. You sent him home? You decided you couldn't work with him?"

Nodding, Franklin replied, "I did. He's a stubborn old man, and I had a promise to keep. I said he'd go home, and I've stuck to that."

"Hmm." Caterina studied his face, sensing there was more to it. "Aren't you afraid that he will try to subvert your creation? Try to make the world see it as his?"

"This did start as my father's invention, and I've made sure he gets the credit for that," he said with a wicked smile.

Caterina raised his chin and smiled at him. "You are a man of strong convictions, and even stronger ideas. Fathers can be dangerous, and incredible disappointments."

"Indeed," replied Franklin.

———————

Maxwell smiled sadly as the ship hands stepped off the boat and started tying it to the Ingleash dock. Hesitating, he took the step and sighed, finally on home soil. The journey had been bittersweet. He appreciated that his son had found a way to send him home, but the sting from their fight had only been made worse with what he'd heard Franklin had been up to. Maxwell had been unable to think of anything other than what would be needed to stop his son from making the worst mistake of his life. Once home, he planned to send a message to his Tub contact immediately so that they knew what was going on.

"Maxwell Watt?" called out a constable walking down the dock, accompanied by two others.

"Constables, I didn't realize I would be getting a special welcome home," replied Maxwell, adjusting his spectacles. "Wait, how did you know I was arriving?"

"Are you related to one Franklin Charles David Watt?" asked the lead constable.

"Yes, that's my son. What's he done? Is he alright? He's rather confused at the moment," said Maxwell, looking at the water. "I hope he's not caused too much trouble."

"Can you confirm that this is his signature?" asked the constable, taking out a piece of paper and showing it to him.

"Yes, why? What's that letter?" Maxwell was confused.

"You're under arrest," said the constable, motioning for the other two to take him.

His face went red with panic. "What? What are you doing? Let go of me."

"You're charged with having worked illegally on one *steam engine* without the approval of the Royal Society for the Collective Progress of Inglea," said the lead constable.

"What? What invention? This is a misunderstanding!"

yelled Maxwell as his hands were put in manacles. "Where did that letter come from? How did you know when I was arriving?"

"It was all in the letter, along with where to search in your home. We found your laboratory, *Mister* Watt. You've been stripped of all rights and privileges of your station. You will face a tribunal in a month's time."

"No!" yelled Maxwell as he was hauled off. *"Franklin!"*

———

Many miles away, Franklin stared at the wall where the present from Caterina hung. The framed design plans had a plaque that he kept running his fingers over: *First Steam Engine - Invented by Franklin C.D. Watt.*

"You going to keep staring at that thing, Franky? I mean, it's just a picture, isn't it?" said Ruffo, straightening up his long coat and frilly sleeves.

"That's the future right there, Ruffo. Let the man... bask in his glory," said Stefano.

"Bask? Geez, big words."

"Hey, if the boss can use it, I can use it. Right, Franky?"

Franklin turned at smiled at them. "Gentlemen, we just put a little dent in history."

"So, what's next?" asked Ruffo.

"Everything, Ruffo. I want everything," said Franklin with a huge grin. "Starting with revenge on Tee Baker and the Yellow Hoods."

CHAPTER THIRTY-ONE

Before the Dawn

Abeland rode the King's-Horse into the empty barn. "Well, that was immensely satisfying. Though I have to say, my mechanical friend, I'd hoped you wouldn't stay silent," he said to it. He dismounted, and, after several minutes of struggling to remember the instructions he'd been given, figured out how to shut it down. The mechanical horse sputtered and shook as it quieted down. "Absolutely amazing." He tapped its nose and turned to Richelle who was staring at him, her mouth agape.

"You leave for a few weeks to gather intelligence and come back with... this? You really are back to your old self," said Richelle with a smile.

"I've been a good boy, I can have nice things again," he replied with a roguish grin. "The contacts you had in the field were invaluable. Invaluable."

Richelle was relieved. It hadn't been hard to find people willing to help them break into Simon St. Malo's study. It was quite another thing to get any information or help regarding the Fare. The news of Marcus' capture had traveled like wildfire, burning their bridges and ties with even some of their staunchest allies. They'd had to make their way, unaided, to the Grand Lab near the border with Southern Teuton.

"Where on Eorth did you find a King's-Horse, let alone one that was working?" she asked, mystified.

"Kar'm. They thought the MCM engine in it was burnt, they didn't know how to reset it. It was damaged, but still worked. It cut my travel back in half. I guess it paid to listen to father go on and on about that mechanical horse statue of his. I never thought it was a real King's-Horse."

"You just... you just waltzed up to Kar'm and took a King's-horse?" she asked.

Abeland nodded, opening one of the saddle bags and taking out his backpack. "You know me. Knock knock, hello? Got anything worth taking? Yes? Thank you."

"I don't believe you," replied Richelle.

"Then feast your eyes on this," he said, taking the unsealed MCM engine out of his backpack and holding it up.

Richelle was speechless. She gently took the six inch square engine from him and marveled at it. "What did it cost you to get?"

"A few good deeds and almost getting myself killed."

"So cheap," replied Richelle, getting a momentary glare from her uncle.

"I'd learned Kar'm had a Fare spy and... told Christina."

"Creangle? You saw her again?" Richelle was surprised. She knew the complicated history between them. "And she let you have this?"

"Not exactly, I'll explain later. Right now I need to know, how's your team doing?"

"I'll show you, come," she said opening a false floor panel, revealing a spiral staircase. She reached around for a crank lantern and brought it to life. "Shall we?"

"After you," replied Abeland, following her lead. "Have you heard anything else from father?"

"After the one Neumatic message, nothing, but it was enough. I got confirmation that he is in Relna. We have one reliable spy there."

"One? Huh," said Abeland. "How the mighty have fallen."

"We will rise again," replied Richelle. "I've got a solid team down here, it won't take me long to build everything else up again. Lessons learned."

"Lessons learned, indeed."

As they descended lower and lower, the air became cool and moist, reminding them both of daring innovation. They'd witnessed some of the most incredible creations in labs such as this one over the years, not all of it working or practical, but all of it rousing and inspiring.

"What can one MCM engine do for us?" asked

Richelle, trying to think how it could be incorporated into their plans.

Abeland chuckled. "If I hadn't had several quiet hours to study it and ask myself that same question, I don't know if it would have hit me. It's not what one of these can do, it's what *several* of these could do, together. If one can power a King's-Horse, then what could, say, a dozen do?"

Stepping onto the creaky wooden floor, Richelle flipped a series of levers on the wall. The chamber filled with the echoes of gears grinding and water rushing until a corridor emerged from the darkness. As dots of light revealed themselves to be wall-mounted lanterns, Abeland smiled.

"You got it working? I'm impressed," said Abeland. "But didn't you have something else to keep you busy?"

Richelle smirked. "We've got a three-quarter size steam engine in testing. I told you having smaller teams would be better. They've been working almost around the clock. It's amazing what a sense of purpose will do, regardless if you're young or old. My team came together quickly, we were lucky. But they also don't need a lot of babysitting. I check in with them every few hours, or when I sense something is off. I needed something to occupy my mind, so that I stayed out of their way and got this working, with a bit of help."

"So, the smaller engine, does it fit in the frame?"

asked Abeland.

"Almost, we need to make it a bit smaller. We were concerned it wouldn't be powerful enough if we made it any smaller. But with MCM engines in series to complement it—"

"Exactly," interrupted Abeland. "All we need is the steam engine to provide the essential lift, and the rest we will handle by MCM. Did I mention I got to see the Skyfallers in action?"

"No," replied Richelle, stopping and wondering.

"They destroyed Kar'm. There was some assistance on the ground, but most of it was done from the air this time. These aren't the same ones that destroyed the palaces of Myke. As I left, I found that they'd been moving them by rail. That's why their limited flight time isn't a factor. But Caterina has the steam engine plans, so it won't be long before she can keep them in the air for days."

Richelle face fell. "Why destroy Kar'm? That's off-limits for... forever."

"I think her message is that nothing is off limits, and that she can get to anyone. Anyone who knew about Kar'm will know they are not safe," replied Abeland.

"That's why you went there, wasn't it? You found out about the attack and wanted to warn Christina," said Richelle.

Abeland stopped and scratched the back of his head.

"Actually, I didn't."

Richelle raised an eyebrow. "Really?"

"I'd learned they had the MCM shortly before catching a satchel of messages. I pretended I'd got them via tube, which she knows nothing about, apparently. Anyway, I did save her life, and that of her father's, before leaving with the MCM and the King's-Horse."

Richelle was impressed, as ever. "You're always so focused."

They stood before the grand double doors at the end of the corridor. They were four times the width of a normal wooden door, and were more than a foot thick. Pulling a hidden lever, they opened, bringing with it a moist underground breeze, the sound of underground rivers and the sounds of their team working away.

As Richelle and Abeland walked up to the huddle of a dozen inventors, scientists and engineers, they stopped and turned to focus on him, like grazing deer hearing a noise.

"I've brought you all a present," boomed Abeland. "Something right out of fairy tale and myth." The team's intense focus was tangible. Abeland pulled out the MCM engine. "One unsealed, mercury-copper-magnetic engine." The intelligible chatter made him smile. "Here," he said, handing it to one of them and climbing on top of a table. He whistled and waved over the people at the rows of dry-docks behind them, busily working away.

Once everyone was gathered, he said, "We all know that my father, Marcus Pieman, has been a man ahead of his time. When he showed me this facility eight years ago, I thought him mad. Why build a fleet of airships that were bodies without a heart and lungs? It seemed like he was pouring a king's ransom into the abyss, money for nothing, but I was wrong. Once we have the steam engine the size we need it, and once we make more of these wonderful miracles," he pointed to the MCM engine one of the inventors was holding above his head, "then we will truly end the Era of the Abominator. Soon, those who stand in our way will fear the skies. We will show what the Fare claims brings the fury of the sky is nothing compared to our Hotaru!"

CHAPTER THIRTY-TWO

THE WORLD, WITH A WINK

"Moving me again? I've not even got half way through my book," said Marcus as he sat up. The jail door clanked closed and soft footfalls approached. For a moment, he wondered if Caterina had tracked him down, despite the best efforts of the royal dignitaries. He still couldn't believe how his begging for meeting with them turned into having the protection of the representatives for the Southern, Eastern, Lower and Independent Kingdoms. If Caterina could turn the tables on *him*, well, he could turn them once again.

He put the book down and stood up, straightening his fine cotton shirt and brown vest. He stroked his clean-shaven chin and glanced around the cozy cell he hadn't even had the chance to call home yet.

"It took me a while to track you down. I don't believe anyone even knows this jail is here, save for those who put you in it. This must be more than four hundred years old," said the approaching figure.

Marcus glanced about. "A fair guess, I'd say. How did you find me, Mister Jenny? It's been a long, long time."

"Someone tried to get a Neumatic message to you. They were sloppy. I happened to be within ear shot when they were caught." Mister Jenny reached into his backpack and pulled out the message, still in its cylinder. He noticed that Marcus' eyepatch was in tatters. "You used the coin, didn't you? The one you keep in your eyepatch."

Marcus smiled, "You knew about that?"

"More of a long running suspicion than an actual guess," replied Mister Jenny.

"You're looking good. It's been far too long," said Marcus.

"It has. And you look remarkably good for a man that was supposed to be dead several times over in the past few weeks alone. But then again, you Piemans are remarkably hard to kill."

Marcus laughed. "Well, I wasn't at my best until an old friend reminded me that everything can change in the blink of an eye. But now, I'm ready to pull the sky down."

———————

The weeks since the attack on his presidential palace had gone by almost entirely unnoticed by Marcus. His dreams were stuck on the moment he'd held Nikolas' unconscious body in his arms, his world destroyed. He'd fought like an animal as Silskin ordered his men to take him before he was eventually knocked out. Since then, he'd been lost in a sea of grief.

It had been a great gamble, taking one of the most brilliant minds and hoping that he would create the next great engine on his own. Nikolas had been Marcus' only true friend, but even so, he'd never managed to bring himself to be honest with Nikolas. When Isabella had died, he no longer knew what Nikolas was up to. He'd waited as long as he could before taking him off the board, concerned that one of his enemies might learn the man had secretly invented something that could tip the scales.

When Ron-Paul Silskin had told him that Nikolas was alive but his mind gone, that he was little more than a demented old man in a decaying shell, it had crushed him. Marcus had risked everything, and in doing so, lost his only friend and his own sense of self.

"You may see him, but only for ten minutes," said the guard, shoving the distraught Marcus into the room with Nikolas and closing the door. It was the second time they'd been together. The first time Nikolas had still been unconscious in his hospital bed. Marcus had confessed and apologized for everything, though it did nothing to ease his burden.

The room housed a fireplace and two large chairs, but little else. Nikolas was seated, counting his fingers. His beard was white and bushy, his hair long and messy.

Marcus' eyes welled up, knowing that his friend would have never allowed himself to be so unkempt.

Nikolas took no notice of Marcus stepping into the room and sitting opposite him. He stared at the painting above the fireplace and mumbled nonsense at it before pointing at his toes angrily. After a moment spent smiling, he returned to counting his fingers.

"They said..." started Marcus. His throat tightened and his eyes filled with tears. "They said you kept calling for me. Are you doing okay?" He leaned into the high-backed chair. "You look... you look..." Tears rolled down his face.

Nikolas' eyes darted around the room and then suddenly stopped. He stared intensely at Marcus' feet. "Nan nan, Marcus. Nan nan no me nan."

Marcus closed his eyes and tried to find meaning in the words, but failed. "Nikolas, I don't understand."

"Bargy no nan. Getto ears, na me. Walls no me ears nan. Da getto ice. Ban dina. Yes?" said Nikolas, getting on all fours and tapping the wooden floor.

Putting his head in his hands, Marcus emotionally broke. He sobbed for minutes as Nikolas babbled and continued to act strangely, crawling around the floor.

Nikolas startled him by shaking him, his eyes intense. "Marcus. Bargy nas. Shakes nan man. Nan nan get ears. Diggo ice bin seen, yes?"

"I don't know what—" and then Marcus stopped

himself. A memory at the back of his mind had twitched. His eyes narrowed as he noticed a pattern. He glanced at the painting and then the opposite wall. "Nan ears hass, no?"

Nikolas shook his head and sat back in his chair. "Bargy bin seen."

"Nan nan," said Marcus.

"*Yes*," replied Nikolas.

A relieved smile crept across Marcus' face, which he casually hid behind a hand. The number of words had a pattern, with nonsense words hiding the occasional one of interest. He stared into Nikolas' eyes and saw the distant look replaced with the fire he'd always known. Nikolas winked, and Marcus chuckled. *You old sneak*, he thought. As Nikolas broke the pattern and went on to count his fingers, Marcus wondered how long he'd be able to keep the act up. It didn't matter, there would be no need for it soon.

When the guard opened the door, he did a double take at Marcus' changed expression. The man before him wasn't the broken one he'd let in, but the man he'd heard legends about. Marcus held a torn eyepatch in his hand and stared intently at the young guard.

"Tell the royal dignitaries that must have arrived by now that I will meet with them in one hour. You will fetch me new clothes and a razor. Also, there's a special message you will send for me."

"Why would I do that?" asked the surprised guard, glancing down the empty hallway.

Marcus stuck out his hand. The guard looked at it and hesitantly shook it. Marcus leaned forward and whispered, "That's a thousand crown coin now in your hand. Either you die when I tell them you were bribed, or you live in the world I'm about to take. Your choice."

Sitting down on the metal bed chained to the back wall, Marcus stared at Mister Jenny. "So, Mister Jenny, what can I do for you?"

"I wanted to let you know that your grandson, Beldon, is alive. He goes by the name Bakon Cochon, and I've been asked to kill him by Caterina. I've got him safely hidden in the Teuton embassy on the other side of Relna. I was wondering if you'd like to join him." Jenny pointed at the cell. "Unless you like the trappings of this new life better?"

Marcus stood up and straightened his vest. "I have to say that, while I appreciate the history, I don't appreciate the decor." He carefully studied Mister Jenny's face. "You have the means for getting me through all of the checkpoints and narrow streets to the embassy? That could very much change things."

"We have to move quickly, though," replied Mister Jenny.

His eyes narrowing, Marcus glanced away. "You know, it took me years to discover why you'd left, that

Gaston Maurice and the little band calling themselves The One True Fare had killed your wife and daughter. And then, to learn that your daughter was actually alive and used as a leash on you, that was heart breaking."

Jenny was clearly caught off guard.

Marcus pushed the cell door open, and then remembering his book, stepped back in and picked it up. "I heard you tried to rescue her once, with nearly disastrous results."

"How could you know?" asked Jenny. "No one knew."

"Nearly no one, but you see, I am Marcus Pieman." He put the still unopened Neumatic cylinder on the bed. "And one thing that people tend to forget is that, more than anything else, my business is to know things." He gestured forward. "Shall we?"

Mister Jenny turned and walk to the jail door when suddenly two shots went off. He slumped to the floor.

Marcus tossed the smoking book aside. He walked over and stared at Jenny in his final moments. "For so long you walked a fine line, but Caterina freed you, and you chose her side. I would have been killed as I fled, and even if I'd made it to the embassy, I don't know who I can trust. My Mister Jenny would have never presumed that I would go with him. That was sloppy, rushed."

"I am going to beat Caterina at her own game." He gave Jenny a wink and stood up, then walked back into his jail cell and closed the door.

THANK YOU
FOR READING THIS BOOK

Reviews are powerful and are more than just you sharing your important voice and opinion, they are also about telling the world that people are reading the book.

Many don't realize that without enough reviews, indie authors are excluded from important newsletters and other opportunities that could otherwise help them get the word out. So, if you have the opportunity, I would greatly appreciate your review.

Don't know how to write a review? Check out **AdamDreece.com/WriteAReview**. Where could you post it? On GoodReads.com and at your favorite online retailer are a great start!

Don't miss out on sneak peeks and news, join my newsletter at: **AdamDreece.com/newsletter**

ABOUT THE AUTHOR

Off and on, for 25 years, Adam wrote short stories enjoyed by his friends and family. Regularly, his career in technology took precedence over writing, so he set aside his dream of one day, maybe, becoming an author.

After a life-changing event, Adam decided to make more changes in his life, including never missing a night of reading stories to his kids again because of work, and becoming an author.

He then wrote a personal memoir (yet unpublished) as every story he tried to write became the story of his life. With that out of the way, he returned to fiction, and with a nudge from his daughter, wrote Along Came a Wolf and created The Yellow Hoods series.

He lives in Calgary, Alberta, Canada with his awesome wife and amazing kids.

Adam blogs about writing and what he's up to at
AdamDreece.com.

He is on Twitter **@AdamDreece** and Instagram
@AdamDreece.

And lastly, feel free to email him at
Adam.Dreece@ADZOPublishing.com

BOOK 5 OF
THE YELLOW HOODS
THE DAY THE SKY FELL

STEAMPUNK MEETS FAIRY-TALE
ADAM DREECE

ISBN: 9780994818485

ADAM DREECE BOOKS

The Man of Cloud 9
ISBN: 9780-994818-430

Tilruna (Season #1)
ISBN: 9781-988746-050

The Wizard Killer, #1-3: 978-0-9948184-5-4,
978-1-988746-01-2, 978-1-988746-03-6

"Harry Potter meets Die
Hard"
–M. Bybee, WereBook.org

"Madmax meets Lord of
the Rings"
–Goodreads.com

A world once at the height
of magical technology and
social order has collapsed.
How and why are the
least of the wizard killer's
worries.